HOT
TEA
AND
MERCY

RAE LASHEA

**THOUGHT
CATALOG**
Books

THOUGHTCATALOG.COM

**THOUGHT
CATALOG
Books**

Published by Thought Catalog Books, an imprint of Thought Catalog, a digital magazine owned and operated by The Thought & Expression Company LLC, an independent media organization founded in 2010 and based in the United States of America. For stocking inquiries, contact stockists@shopcatalog.com.

Produced by Chris Lavergne and Noelle Beams
Art direction and design by KJ Parish
Creative editorial direction by Brianna Wiest
Circulation management by Isidoros Karamitopoulos

thoughtcatalog.com | shopcatalog.com

First Edition, Limited Edition Pressing

Printed in China.
ISBN 978-1-949759-57-0

CHAPTER ONE

Shandell

"HOT TEA AND MERCY. Hot tea and Mercy. Please please please get me hot tea and Mercy," Shandell O'Brien whispered through whimpers as tears streamed down her face.

She lay on her left side in a fetal position in incomprehensible discomfort, wishing she could turn over but fearing the agony that she would experience as pain shot through the right side of her abdomen, radiated up her left thigh, and settled excruciatingly in the middle of her rectum where the tumor of inconceivable size rested. Nestled comfortably in the space that it decided to inhabit seven years ago, seemingly as a hemorrhoid; it grew and grew, folding over itself and covering most of Shandy's butthole so much so that it brought tears to her eyes whenever the thought of moving her bowels came to mind.

Upon the realization by Shandell and the doctors that the culprit of all her grief was colorectal cancer and that the only way to eliminate the

tumors would be through chemotherapy and radiation, Shandell took a
bold and courageous stance and decided that she would not undergo the
toxic treatment but rather use alternative and holistic methods to cure
herself of the impending doom and havoc that colon cancer can and has
wreaked on the lives of so many before her, including her grandmother
at the age of eighty-seven, her father at the age of seventy-four, and most
recently, her cousin at the tender age of fifty-six. At fifty-three years old,
Shandy planned on beating cancer, in fact annihilating it to smithereens.

"Hot tea and Mercy, hot tea and Mercy, hot tea and Mercy", she
whispered through tear-filled whimpers, which no one heard as she laid
on an air mattress in her one-bedroom apartment in an East Side housing project in Atlanta, Georgia. It wasn't that she did not have any family,
she just chose to distance herself from them over the years. Embarrassed
about her situation, not wanting to hear the many taunts against her decision not to undergo chemo, and a general disdain for the fact that no one
else got pregnant at the age of sixteen and dropped out of high school,
Shandy saw herself as a black sheep; a poor black sheep that was at the
mercy of public assistance, public housing, and Medicaid.

Shandy was a beautiful girl with long curly hair, brown skin, and
a big smile full of large white teeth that she wanted to have molded for
her future dentures. She had a clear complexion marked only by a smat-
tering of milk chocolate brown freckles on each of her cheeks. She was
5'7" and had slender fingers with strong, pretty nails. Shandy did not
feel pretty and spent most of her life depressed for reasons unknown to
anyone, including herself. She felt unloved, unhappy, underappreciated,
and undersexed. Worst of all, she battled with her weight which always
seemed to win.

She was on the larger size all of her life, reaching two hundred and
ninety pounds at her highest weight. She always felt that people would
appreciate her better if she was skinnier. That she would be respected
more. That she would be able to enjoy tantamount sexual experiences
if she was smaller. Over the past three years, Shandy's family watched
her wither down to a mere one hundred and twenty-five pounds. With
sunken cheeks and a fragile frame, everyone had encouraged her to get the
chemotherapy treatment that the doctors were offering, but when Shandy

looked in the mirror all she could see was the small body she had always wanted. If she could just get rid of the illness, she thought, she could start living the life and having the sex that she had always wanted. Despite the pain, Shandy secretly appreciated the disease because it made her what no one and nothing else could: thin.

CHAPTER TWO

Nella

"YOU ARE BIGGER THAN YOUR JOB, JIM. You are bigger than your career. You are even, believe it or not, bigger than the entire profession. You, my dear, just have to believe in yourself and have the confidence to move forward boldly, courageously. You can and will find another way to make money. You just have to have faith and rely on your talents, abilities, interests, and experiences. The key is knowing what all of those things are and where they intersect," Dr. Nella allowed a long pause to idle in the air so that her words could sink into the head, heart, and spirit of her client. "That concludes our session for today. Call to schedule your next session once you have landed a new job."

Nella knew that the pain of not seeing her would encourage, inspire, and indeed force her client to find new employment faster than anything else could. She hoped he would still do all of the things that she told him to, but in the meanwhile, he had bills that needed to be paid. Besides, she could not conscientiously accept two hundred dollars of his money for another hour, knowing he was unemployed.

"Thank you, doctor."

"My pleasure."

Nella had always had a keen sense of exactly what she needed to say to people to help them feel good. This quality, along with her beautiful Latina features, a face from Spain and a body from Columbia, proved to be a great asset to her household as she traipsed alongside her husband, often unwillingly, as he schmoozed company CEOs in attempts to gain their trust and their accounts. An information technology project manager is as good a job as any; however, with four languages under his belt and meticulous attention to detail, Paulo was a coveted manager and could land international accounts that paid him handsomely and sent them on trips around the world.

Ten years his junior and married just out of undergrad, Nella found this life fun and exciting. Eight years into the marriage; however, at the age of thirty and experiencing a quarter-life crisis, Nella found herself angry, lonely, and feeling worthless. Though beautiful and smart, all she was was Paulo's wife, and that thought began to sicken her. Perhaps it was his cheating that began to take a toll on her, the whispers of friends and family behind her back about his behavior and infidelity started to become unbearable. Once Nella finally decided that she needed her own identity, she went back to school, which he paid for, and got a degree in psychiatry. She became a doctor, opened a small practice, and soon became well-known for getting people back on track when they believed, whether true or not, that their world was falling apart.

In practice for ten years now, at the age of forty-eight, her one and only five-year-old son is her world, her joy, her Angel. Nella works long hours Mondays through Fridays from eight a.m. until eight p.m. and Saturdays from nine in the morning until two in the afternoon and she often finds herself exhausted. Dark circles have begun to shadow underneath her eyes and she hears the whisper of voices in her head saying quit, divorce, leave it all behind. She keeps forward momentum with three cups of coffee a day and quiets those voices with beer, vodka, and tequila sometimes. At other times, rum or whiskey do the trick.

Nella hadn't worn her wedding ring or slept with Paulo since Angel was three years old. Already feeling embarrassed for what family and friends seemed to have figured out, she endured the snickers and sneers that tainted the air at birthday parties and family reunions, but nothing could have prepared or mortified her more than rushing her three-year-old son who had a one hundred two fever to the doctor in the middle of the day on her lunch break to find Paulo's car at the far corner of the parking lot. With a hot and feverish baby in her arms, she walked over to inspect it and make sure that her eyes were not playing tricks on her. To her ultimate dismay, she saw Paulo screwing the doctor's office receptionist in the backseat. With tears in her eyes and a temperature nearly surpassing that of Angel's, she took the baby to the emergency room to be treated. She never stepped foot into that doctor's office again and even though they shared the same king-sized bed, Nella slept on one side and Paulo on the other, never meeting in the middle.

As the stress of her growing practice and maintaining their large ranch-style house in North Las Vegas began to weigh on her, Nella found it necessary to hire live-in help who could double as a nanny when Angel was home and a housekeeper when he was at school. Requiring that the person they hired was bilingual so that Angel could be fluent in both languages, they found Priscilla, a forty-year-old single mother of one daughter who she was desperately trying to put through college.

CHAPTER THREE

Priscilla

BORN IN COSTA RICA TO A TICA MOTHER and an American father, her parents left her in San Pedro with her maternal grandparents to live and work in the United States, somewhat forgetting about her and having three more American-born children. When her grandmother died at the age of sixty-five, her seventy-year-old abuelo went to live with one of his other children. Priscilla moved to the U.S. to be with her parents who left when she was two, and siblings whom she had never met. She was fourteen years old and didn't speak a word of English.

Priscilla was miserable at home with five people who she didn't know and with whom she couldn't communicate. Though her mother spoke Spanish fluently, she refused to, under the auspice that Priscilla would learn English. It seemed to Priscilla that her mother was ashamed of her culture and heritage and did her best to separate from being a Tica. She dressed like an American, she talked like an American, she cooked like an American, and she acted like an American. Priscilla missed her grandparents deeply and just wanted to be back in Costa Rica where the food, people, and language were familiar.

With trepidation, Priscilla entered high school in Las Vegas and quickly found her niche. With other Spanish-speaking schoolmates, socializing was not as hard as she had imagined it would be. School work was a different story and so she failed English, Science, Social Studies, and Math. She would have passed gym if she had changed into her gym shorts but being very curvaceous and a bit overweight, she was embarrassed by her body and remained clothed in her baggy jeans and tee shirts. Priscilla was quiet in class and purposely flew under the radar. She signed her report cards for the four years that she was in high school, never fully graduating to the next grade and always having to attend summer school. Her parents worked a lot and had their hands full with her younger siblings, so as long as Priscilla helped around the house and was home to babysit when they needed her to, they didn't get on her case about grades, assuming she would do better once she learned English.

At the age of eighteen, and now mostly fluent in English, Priscilla was just going to the eleventh grade. All of her friends graduated and though she was popular among the students who were there, Priscilla had to decide whether or not she would become a super senior and remain in school for another two years. While idly walking from the park one day, lost in her thoughts about school and friends and the completion of summer school, an olive-green Cadillac pulled up alongside her. Inside of it was a tall, thin, semi-attractive man with a gold chain and dangling Jesus piece around his neck.

He rolled down the passenger side window and whistled to Priscilla who was jolted from her thoughts and turned to look at him. "How's it going there, sweetness? I'd sure like to have you come and work for me."

Sweetness. Those words had never been uttered to Priscilla before who began to blush and feel tingly inside. Some of the boys at school used to try to touch her butt or breasts, but no one ever seriously showed any interest in her and never in a way that made her feel good. This was a new experience, a new feeling. Priscilla decided it was a nice feeling.

"Hop in pretty lady. We can go talk over some ice cream. If you're interested, you work. If you're not, you got some ice cream on me."

Priscilla didn't feel scared or threatened by any means. She just stood there looking at him deciding if she wanted chocolate or vanilla. Ice cream was a treat in her home and here it was being offered to her on a silver platter. He sat there, patiently waiting, not sure if she would get in or not, but knowing from his twenty-eight years on the planet and his ten years of pimping experience that young women could easily be enticed by sweet things; he was offering two: money and ice cream.

"What's your favorite flavor, sweetness? Butter pecan or Cookies and Cream?"

That was it. Cookies and Cream is what she wanted and with that, she walked over and put her hand on the door handle.

"Oh yeah sweetness, hop in, get comfortable," he unlocked the car door and Priscilla opened it. "My name is Burger. You can call me B, Burg, Burger, or Mac," he chuckled. "What's your handle?"

"Huh?" Priscilla looked up from the seatbelt that she had just fastened.

"Your name, what do you want me to call you?" he asked.

"Just keep calling me Sweetness," she said very matter of factly. Priscilla wasn't flirting or being cute and didn't even realize that she was being ushered in as a prostitute in training. She just liked being called Sweetness and wanted to continue to be referred to as that for as long as it would last. Burger drove her home after ice cream where she packed a small duffle bag and left her family a note. It read:

Found a job elsewhere. Will be in touch. —Pri

She never was. Sweetness lasted for three years as she hoed for Burger, who taught her everything she knew about sex, pimping, prostituting, life in the streets, alcohol, drugs, addiction, sobriety, domestic violence, and homelessness. She loved Burger as a man, a father, a provider, a protector, and once she got pregnant by him, as her baby daddy. It was only through a miracle that she left the stroll.

A few weeks after her baby girl was born, Burger wanted Priscilla to get back to work. When she wouldn't he beat her. Having never been hit by a man, she was pretty shaken up but resolved that that would be the only time in his life that he would do that to her. She agreed to get back out on the street once she stopped bleeding "down there".

Slicing through some potatoes to make potato salad on a Sunday afternoon, Priscilla realized that she would either have to kill Burger or leave him since she'd rather die than start hoeing again. Looking at the knife and contemplating approaching him from behind as he unsuspectingly watched basketball, three things occurred to her. First, she loved him and did not want him dead. Second, he was the father of her child, and she did not want her daughter to grow up fatherless. The third and most important reason was that losing her freedom for killing Burger would be pointless since being in jail would take her away from her baby girl.

"Can you run to the store and get me some mayonnaise for this potato salad," she asked him.

"Get it your damn self," he answered, just as she knew he would.

"Give me the money then big daddy," she stroked his ego.

He gave her a twenty and told her to grab a carton of Cookies and Cream. *Funny*, she thought. *I'm leaving the same way I came in.* She took the money and put the baby in her stroller. "Might as well let her get some sun," she said as she strapped her in.

Burger didn't pay Sweetness much mind as she fiddled with the carriage. "Oh, give me another twenty so I can get some diapers. I don't want to have to go out again anymore this week," she said nonchalantly.

Without glancing her way, Burger pulled out a twenty-dollar bill and handed it to her, never taking his eyes off the television. With the baby bag tucked neatly under a blanket in the undercarriage and Priscilla's i.d. card, money, phone, and a few pair of clean underwear hidden inside, she walked out the door to the corner gas station just as she had run it through her mind one hundred times the night before. There she grabbed a cab to the furthest shelter that forty dollars could take her and began to figure out a new life for herself and her sweet baby girl, Milagro.

CHAPTER FOUR

NELLA GAVE PRISCILLA A TOUR of the house. She had her own small bedroom with a twin-sized bed, small desk and stool, a wooden armoire, and a small bathroom. It was part of the house, though slightly off to the side, past the laundry room and adjacent to the two-car garage.

"This is where you'll stay in your free time and during all family functions. Of course, you can eat meals with us, but if you'd rather eat in your room, that is perfectly fine and preferred. Except for breakfast, which you are responsible for feeding Angel. You'll also make his lunch for school. His room is on the other side near us. You will play with him there and make sure to put all of his toys away each evening and put his pajamas on before dinner. Dinner is at 7:30 each night and Paulo cooks. The dishwasher is loaded after each meal and runs every two to three days, depending on its fullness. You can put the dishes in the cabinets once they are clean.

"Our bed will need to be made each morning and our sheets and comforter washed and changed weekly. There is also a guest room on that end that should be kept dusted and tidy. Of course, you are responsible for keeping your room clean and washing your own clothes. We have a washing machine and dryer. You will wash, fold, and put away our clothes weekly. Paulo's shirts should be ironed and hung. My suits are taken to the dry cleaners on Cheyenne Avenue on Thursdays. You can pick them up on Saturday when you take Angel to his swimming lessons. Please clean all three of the bathrooms twice a week and of course vacuum, sweep, mop, dust, and clean mirrors as necessary. Cleaning supplies are in the laundry room near your bedroom, as is the iron and ironing board.

"You work Monday to Friday from seven-thirty to seven-thirty and on Saturdays from eight to three. You have Sundays off and when we vacation you will accompany us, all expenses paid. Two thousand five hundred is the salary we discussed over the phone, with room and board included. Paulo goes to the supermarket every Sunday; you can accompany him or give him a short list of anything that you may need him to pick up. Any questions?" Nella gave Priscilla all of the details she needed to fulfill the job description that she had accepted through the Nanny Match app for domestic help.

Priscilla had bounced around over the past seventeen years, taking her daughter with her from relationship to relationship as each one provided the housing, support, and security they needed. She was with Jose for three years, then Mario for five, Felix lasted for four years and then back with Jose for two, and Mario again for the last four. Of course, Priscilla loved these men, but the relationships became more and more transactional as the years went on. She cooked well and kept a tidy house. She knew all the tricks to keep a man satisfied and interested in bed. In return, she and her daughter had a place to live, food to eat, spending money, transportation, and a decent life. As Milagro graduated high school and prepared to go to college; however, Priscilla knew she couldn't count on these men to pay her daughter's tuition, and frankly, she was tired of being attached.

With no high school diploma, no job experience and no money, Priscilla's best bet was to get a live-in job cooking and cleaning and raising someone else's child, just as she had been doing all these years with her own. She thought it would be on her terms, but as she quickly realized, living under Nella's roof didn't grant her the freedom she had hoped for. In the meantime, the money was better than she had ever experienced, and Angel was a sweet - albeit spoiled - little boy. It would be some time before she realized that she was being underpaid, but for now, she had a roof over her head, food in her tummy, and Milagro's tuition was up-to-date. She couldn't be more satisfied.

CHAPTER FIVE

～～～

"NELLA, PASE LAS PAPAS PORFA," Paulo always spoke in Spanish so that Angel could learn both languages fluently. "Nella, porfa. NELLA!"

Nella looked up and then passed Paulo the potatoes slowly and with disinterest. She was oftentimes much better at masking her disdain, but today she was particularly upset with Paulo for the conversation that she needed to have with him. Unlike most women who would be nice to their husbands to get what they wanted, Nella was just the opposite. She offered a coldness that pierced through Paulo's heart and head. He loved her greatly despite his infidelities and wanted so badly to please her. She knew that he would do anything to make her happy and therefore utilized drama and theatrics to play to his sensitivities and get her way. It was exhausting for the both of them, but it was a dance they had perfected over the last twenty years and neither of them saw a need in changing it or had the mental or emotional strength to.

"My sister is coming to stay with us," Nella blurted out right before she pushed a forkful of mashed potatoes into her mouth.

"Que? No."

"Si."

"Que es esto? What is this? No, no way."

Paulo was not trying to hear the bad news of Nella's sister coming to stay with them, again. Marcella had done it once before after her first divorce and it was a nightmare. She didn't pay rent, she didn't buy groceries, she did not clean, she hardly cooked, she was not considerate, and she did not cooperate.

"She is divorcing and needs…"

"Again? What a surprise." Paulo could not refrain from commenting.

"So what? She is coming and that's it."

"That is not it, Nella. You cannot just sit here and tell me I have to take care of your sister."

"You don't have to take care of her."

"She can't take care of herself."

"She is an adult and doesn't need you to take care of her."

"Then why is she coming to live here in my house?"

"Your house or our house?"

"It is our house that I paid for and we live in. She did this once before and didn't contribute anything while she was here."

"She doesn't have to. We make more money than her."

"I'm not talking about money. I'm talking about anything. Help around the house. Cooking. Nothing."

"We have help now."

"But we didn't have it before. And that is not the point. She can take advantage."

"How is she taking advantage if we make more than her?"

"If we make more than her and she doesn't have to contribute or cooperate then we are taking care of her."

"I am taking care of her, not you."

"What? That doesn't even make sense. I take care of you."

"You take care of me? You think you take care of me?"

"I know I do. What do you pay for? Massages and jewelry and shopping and shoes. You keep all of your money. I pay for everything."

"I am the queen, of course, that is the way it works."

"Then I am the king."

"That's not how it goes."

"That's how it should go."

"Well, it doesn't. Thank you and good night." Nella gave Paulo a small peck on his cheek, scooped up Angel and walked away, leaving Paulo to finish his dinner alone and clean up the kitchen while he chewed on the fact that Marcella would be moving in with them, again.

CHAPTER SIX

Paulo

PAULO WAS BORN IN NICARAGUA. Having gotten married right out of high school at the age of eighteen, Paulo's mom and dad seemed to have had the perfect relationship. They weren't rich, but they were comfortable. Paulo's dad left the house every morning at seven a.m. to go to work at a resort at the edge of town. His mom stayed home. With a ton of education in being a Latina woman, Paulo's mom kept a clean home and raised seven beautiful children. He was the eldest. Paulo's dad's dinner was always on the table and his clothes were always laundered by hand and hung to dry on the line in the hot Central American sun.

Paulo's parents had an excellent relationship. His mom never argued with his dad and his dad faithfully went to work, came home, played with his children, paid the bills, and loved his wife. It took Paulo by surprise the morning after his Junior High School graduation when his mother told him to get dressed so that they could go speak to the principal of his new school.

"That's not how it works, Madre. I just show up at my new school, the high school, at the beginning of the year. I will get my classes then," Paulo protested.

Paulo had a carefree attitude towards life. His parents doted on him as their first son. He was a smart kid but didn't apply himself more than he needed to. He was given free rein to go outside, play with his friends, and be a couch potato, never having to do chores or lift a finger around the house.

"Get dressed, we must go now," Paulo's mother had a look of panic on her uncharacteristically made-up face. She wore a fitted white skirt with a short-sleeved light-weight black shirt that had both a frilly and plunging neckline. She put on comfortable but cute black sandals and huffed at Paulo to hurry up.

Though confused, Paulo got dressed and walked with his mother to what was to become his new high school after the summer break. The two walked into the school building and found the main office, where his mother requested to speak with the principal. Once inside his office, Paulo's mother explained to the principal that it would be extremely important for Paulo to be placed in the classes that would allow him to get a scholarship for college, go to an excellent college, and get a good job that he could take care of his family with.

"Well Mrs. Palma, it doesn't exactly work like that. Paulo will take the basic classes just like everyone else. His grades will determine where he goes to college and the college will determine whether or not they want to give him a scholarship to attend."

Without flinching, Paulo's mom spoke clear and steady. "Paulo's father left us this morning. He is not coming back. I have seven children, no job, and no education. Paulo is now the man of the family. He will have to take care of his younger brothers and sisters. I'm young and will figure it out for now, but Paulo will have to take over in the next 10 years. I need your help in making him responsible. For making him a man."

Hearing the news for the first time, Paulo sat there with tears welling up in his eyes. He did not know anything about his dad leaving. He was even more uncertain of how to be a man and how he would take care of his family.

The principal stared at Paulo's mom with a look of sympathy. He then looked at Paulo. A fleeting flicker flashed across his face, a seeming twinkle in his eye, that only Paulo registered.

"Have him come here one week from this Monday. He will join our janitorial staff and work for the summer; cleaning classrooms, painting walls, and fixing desks and chairs. That should give him some experience in learning a trade and also some money to bring home for the summer. He will have to take classes and do well in his subjects just like everyone else, but there is a program here called The Einsteins. Ten students are chosen to participate each year. You have to be a senior, so when he gets to that point, we can put him there. Those students are very good in science, technology, or math and get scholarships or internships. He'll be in line for that as long as he keeps good grades."

"Excellent, thank you. How can I repay you?" Paulo's mother was prepared to do anything to ensure her son's success and the survival of her family.

"You do not have to repay someone for being a good mother. Tell you what, Paulo. Whenever I need to paint a wall or cut some grass at my house, I'll let you know. You can come there and make additional money to help out at home."

"Thank you. Mr. Vasquez. Thank you so much. Paulo will be here, one week from Monday. Thank you so much," Paulo's mom was beaming and shaking the principal's hand profusely. She gathered her purse and tapped Paulo's shoulder for him to get up, though he was still in a daze.

Paulo's mom was relieved that the principal did not ask anything of her, though she was willing to give it all. At this point, all it would cost was a weekend or two of Paulo doing yard work for Mr. Vasquez. As a bonus, he would be working for the summer and making some money. Mrs. Palma felt confident that Paulo would do well in school and earn the Einstein internship. Unfortunately, the fact of the matter was that there were four years between now and then and she needed to figure out a way to make money, pay bills, and feed all seven of her children. She could not believe that after fifteen years of marriage, her husband woke up that morning and told her he was leaving to pursue his dream of mariachi.

He had met a gringa at the resort where he worked as a landscaper who told him she would buy him a guitar and show him the world. Since he could not pass up what he described as 'the opportunity of a lifetime,' he took the gringa up on her offer. He quit his job the evening before, came home and ate dinner, made love to his high school sweetheart one last time before bed, then packed a small suitcase of clothes in the morning and left after a quick conversation over coffee and bread.

Never being one to argue, Paulo's mom sat as still as a statue, frozen by the words that were coming out of her husband's mouth. She said nothing and it was only when he quietly closed the door behind him that the first tear rolled down her cheek. She cleared the table of their breakfast dishes and went on to scramble eggs for the children to eat when they woke up. She got dressed as pretty as she remembered how, plastered her face with make-up, put on her rosary, and prayed to God. As Paulo and his mom walked out of the school, she knew God had answered her prayers.

Paulo stayed up all night, deep in thought and reminiscent of the resolve that he had come to all of those years ago to be willing to do anything that would help his mom and his family. He worked hard with the janitorial staff that summer, which made it possible for his family to eat and for all of the kids to have school supplies and new shoes. He hadn't gone to work at the home of his new principal, but once school started he would shake his hand or be the recipient of a thumbs up or eye wink if he ever happened to inadvertently pass him in the hallway or see him in a class-room or the cafeteria.

By the end of the summer, Paulo's mother had found a job at a bakery where she worked early mornings baking bread and cinnamon rolls. She also worked in the afternoons as a launderer, washing sheets by hand for a tourist hostel. She made enough money for the family to survive and in the evenings, she would cook extra food and sell fried chicken or fish plates to neighbors at eight dollars a meal. On Saturdays, she would make her signature Peruvian-style ceviche which sold out each weekend.

Paulo got good grades in every class each semester. His sisters began to pick up the slack around the house, doing dishes and washing clothes since their mother could hardly get out of bed on Sundays. Paulo watched as his mother's face lost its color and began to sag with wrinkles. By the time he was a junior in high school, her hands had taken on a prune-like look. Her nails were chipped and yellowing, and her hair had begun to both thin and gray simultaneously. He felt sorry for his mother. Watching her shoulder the weight of seven kids without ever complaining was a testament to her love and dedication for her family. Neither he nor any of his siblings ever went hungry or without shoes. Every one of his brothers and sisters went to their graduations and plans for an upcoming quinceanera were never foiled. Paulo knew he had to do everything right to become a man and take care of his family. He had been determined to be the man that his father proved not to be.

Paulo became a permanent member of the summer janitorial staff each year, which helped a great deal at home and made it possible for him to focus on his studies throughout the school year. At the end of his junior year, he began to think about how he would be able to pay for the next year's senior activities, the prom, his yearbook, and graduation. He also realized that if he left for college, the entire financial burden would be on his mother. He planned to apply for The Einstein's senior internship as soon as school started and ask the principal if he could work part-time after school with the janitors. He would get accepted to the internship and work his ass off to prove that he was the right man for the scholarship and earn a full ride through college.

Paulo ended his junior year at the top of his class and as a viable candidate for valedictorian. He was excited about his prospects and had a positive outlook on life. With a college scholarship and a perfect grade point average, he could attend any school he wished, maybe even go to Oxford. He was happy and he allowed himself to daydream about what the future held. He would enjoy the next few weeks off before starting work with the janitors at school. To make the most of his time, Paulo decided that he would find out if Mr. Vasquez had any extra work or odd jobs that he could tackle over the next few weeks or on summer weekends. Paulo was determined to continue to be the best man in his mother's life. He was her sunshine and she was his everything.

CHAPTER SEVEN

~~~~~

"CAN YOU HELP WITH MY BAGS?"

"Aye, Marcella. Good to see you. Come in, sit down. Paulo. Can you help get her stuff out of the car?" Nella sounded both happy and exasperated as she rushed around the house to make sure everything was perfect for her younger sister. She had fixed up the guest bedroom and also ordered pizza from Marcella's favorite Italian restaurant, which would be there in the next twenty minutes. She fawned and fussed over her sister who was freshly divorced and who Nella was happy to have there with her. "Paulo!"

Paulo slowly got off of the dining table stool that he was sitting on while he watched sports on the small flatscreen television that was mounted high on the wall of the kitchen. He dragged himself across the living room and out of the door, through the driveway, and to the sidewalk where Marcella's ex-husband was sitting in the driver's seat of his Explorer. Paulo walked over to the driver's side window and shook his hand.

"Paulo, ¿que tal?" Manuel greeted him.

"Bien Manuel, ¿y tu?" Paulo responded.

"I am well, thanks. Just dropping off your sister-in-law."

"So it didn't work out, huh?"

"Not quite like I had hoped."

"It never does, Manuel. It never does. Do you want to come in for a beer or a glass of wine? Some coffee?"

"No, I'm fine, thanks. Going to grab something to eat and head in."

"Nella ordered pizza from Sammy's. You are more than welcome to stay and eat."

"No thanks, Paulo. I have plans. Maybe another time."

"Okay, well, let me just grab Marcella's things and let you be on your way."

"Okay, it is everything in the back seat and the trunk. I'd help you, but truly, she has already gotten everything that she is going to get out of me, so."

"No problem, jefe." Paulo took all of the suitcases, plastic bags, plastic cartons, and cardboard boxes out of the car and set them on the driveway. He waved goodbye to Manuel who drove off hastily. Paulo carried the largest suitcase through the front door, walked past the ladies on the couch, and took it back to the guest bedroom. He slowly began bringing in all of the items with no help from the women and when the last of the boxes were placed in the guestroom, he went to lay down in his own bed.

"Paulo, the pizza is here," Nella skipped into the room eating a slice of pizza that included sausage, ham, bacon, and pepperoni on top.

"¿Que tipo?" He asked wearily.

"Meat lovers."

"Aiy Nella, you know I don't eat all of that junk. Did you get any veggie?"

"No, this is Marcella's favorite."

"So, it's all about Marcella?"

"I like it too."

"And what about me, Nella? What about your husband?"

"I'm going to send Angel in for bed." Nella turned around, dimmed the light, and left the room. She did not want to argue with Paulo and was not going to let his sour attitude ruin the joy she was feeling about having her sister there with her.

"Angel, kiss tia and go to bed. Daddy is waiting for you."

Having picked off all of the meat and only eating the cheese and bread from his pizza, Angel gave his aunt Marci a kiss and went to bed.

"Buenas noches mi amor."

"Good night mommy, I lub you."

"Oh, que lindo. He is such a good boy," Marcella said.

"Yes, he is. I am so lucky. If it wasn't for him, I would not be here."

"I know, hermana. I hope I am as lucky to have as beautiful a baby as you do."

"You will one day, you are still young."

"No, I mean, I hope my baby is as beautiful as Angel is."

"What? Wait. What? You? Now? Baby?" Nella couldn't speak in full sentences as she attempted to wrap her head around what Marcella was saying.

"Yes, hermana. Estoy embarazada. I am pregnant."

"Oh my goodness, gracious. Yes! Congratulations."

"Thank you. Yes, I know. But don't tell anyone, please. It is our secret for now."

"Of course, of course. But this calls for a celebration. This calls for vino."

"I can't drink wine," Marcella laughed.

"It's only a little," Nella chuckled as she retrieved two wine glasses from the cabinet.

"I'll just take some soda."

"Okay. Well, more for me. Is it Manuel's?"

"No."

"Que?"

There was so much to talk about and so much to whisper. The two drank and talked and laughed and shared secrets until they got sleepy and retired to bed.

CHAPTER EIGHT

Shandell

"I DON'T KNOW WHY YOU LEFT in the first place. You should have never left," Shandell's mother yelled into the phone.

"Ma, I don't need you to yell at me. I left because I was better, but now I'm back to being sick. I just need you to find me that doctor's number, please."

"How am I supposed to know where that doctor's number is?"

"Just look! Look at my paperwork or in the drawers of the desk in the office. Worst case, go down to the hospital where I used to get my treatment and ask them. I need to speak to her. Please!"

"Okay, I'll see what I can do. I'll try to find it and get back to you. How are you, anyway?"

"Not good, Ma. I'm sick. I'm hurting. The tumors have come back. And they're worse than ever. I'm in a bad way right now."

"Well, you should have never left. You were getting better, and you had people to take care of you. I can't do anything for you there. And Kayla has got them boys!"

"I'll be fine Ma. Don't worry. Just get me that number."

"You should have never left."

"Okay thanks, Ma. I love you. Talk to you tomorrow."

Shandell attempted to turn on her side and winced in pain. She was alone, in pain. Her daughter lived right across the lot but rarely came over. Shandell wasn't mad though. She knew Kayla was busy working and getting the boys to and from school. She was cooking dinner and making lunches and bathing them and putting them to bed. But damn, she could bring them over and cook there, couldn't she?

Shandell began to reminisce on her childhood. It was unhappy. Her mother and father were always yelling at each other; the walls reverberating their threats. Late night parties in their apartment, cigarette smoke wafting into her bedroom. The sight of glasses with smidges of whiskey left on the card table the next morning when it was quiet and everyone was gone, her parents still asleep.

The only thing worse than her parents being together was after they separated. Her mother was always gone, partying and hanging in the streets, disappearing for days at at time. Her dad fought for custody and won. Shandell was twelve and loved living with her father. A few years later, he met a younger woman from the Philippines. At the age of forty-five, Shandell's father decided to remarry. Shandell was sixteen and adamantly against their union. She refused to go to the wedding right up until the last minute. With nothing to wear, Shandell went to the church and sat outside on the steps in jeans and a yellow tee-shirt waiting for her father to say I do, believing she would lose him forever.

It was that summer, just six months later, that she got pregnant by Sergio, a senior at her Brooklyn high school. It was her first time having sex. She was embarrassed and scared and didn't know what to do. She spoke to the guidance counselor at school who called her father in for a meeting. Together, the counselor and Shandell informed her dad that she was pregnant. He was understanding, but mad. Just married and not knowing what to do with a pregnant teenage daughter who did not quite get along with his new wife, he sent her back to live with her mother, Mrs. Wright.

Shandell loved her father but came to resent him for sending her back. Not because it was a bad living situation, but because her mother took Shandell's son just days after she had given birth. Mrs. Wright gave him away to her sister, Shandell's aunt, who had never had children of her own. Shandell's aunt and her husband Raphael adopted the baby and named him Raphael, Jr. They raised him as their own son and moved to Chihuahua, Mexico, where Raphael was originally from.

Shandell didn't see Raphael, Jr. again until eighteen years later when her aunt died, and she attended the funeral. Unsure of what to say to her son, she avoided him until he came up to her at the end of the service.

"I know who you are."

"You do?"

"You are my biological mother." Tall and handsome, he bent down to hug her and whispered in her ear, "And I will never forgive you."

He walked away and left Shandell standing there, stunned. There was so much she wanted to say; needed to say, but she couldn't. She didn't. She was frozen. Her mouth became dry and her legs heavy. She felt stuck, like she couldn't move. It was like she was standing in a pile of quicksand, slowly sinking, with no way out.

"What are you just standing there for?" Her mother appeared out of nowhere. "Everyone is getting in cars to go to the gravesite and you're just standing there like a dummy."

In an instant, Shandell began crying. "Oh, I'm sorry, dear. You miss your auntie. I know this is hard for everyone." Mrs. Wright put her arm around Shandell's shoulders and guided her toward the exit. Not wanting to be touched, but happy someone was there to hold her up and get her moving, Shandell allowed her mom to direct her steps to the cars outside. Shandell got in one and sat quiet and teary-eyed. She stared out the window until they got to the gravesite where she refused to get out, opting instead to stay in the car and fall asleep. She didn't wake up until she was back in front of her aunt's house and everyone was gone.

Maybe it was the poor example that she had for a mother, or the missed opportunity at motherhood with her first son that turned her into an indifferent parent. She had Kayla ten years later at the age of twenty-six with a handsome man who had a good job, his own place, and a car. Shandell decided to leave when Roger began to call her names. Fat pig, cow, moose, biggums. They were all just too much for Shandell to handle once Kayla could understand. It hadn't bothered her all that much when he called her names, considering she had been verbally abused by her mother for many years, but as Kayla got older, Shandell refused to let her daughter be around someone who was verbally abusive towards women, fearing it would negatively affect her self-esteem. When Kayla turned four, Shandell left the comfortable Brooklyn brownstone that they lived in with Roger and moved to a one-room rental in a nice house in a bad neighborhood in Queens, New York.

It was an interesting dichotomy, however, because while Shandell refused to let Roger verbally abuse them, she never missed an opportunity to physically slap Kayla. Go to sleep, slap. Eat your food, slap. Get dressed, slap. Who spilled the juice? Slap. Take a shower, slap. Iron the clothes, slap. Do the dishes, slap. Cook the food, slap. Make your bed, slap. There was nothing that didn't deserve a slap and Kayla found herself walking on eggshells and wincing every time her mother lifted an arm. Shandell might not have remembered it, but the memories resurfaced for Kayla every time she slapped one of her own three boys.

CHAPTER NINE

Kayla

SHE REMAINED WITH HER MOTHER UNTIL she was eighteen and then went to live with her dad, which lasted two years; just long enough to save the checks she was acquiring through her job at Castles fast food restaurant. On her twenty-first birthday, with money from her grandmother and the blessing of her father, Kayla boarded a Greyhound bus for a nineteen-hour ride to Atlanta. Eight years and three kids later, she lived in a public housing complex on the East End with her sons' father, who was often in the studio laying tracks for his up-and-coming and highly imagined rap career. Her mother moved in across the lot last year after undergoing two rounds of chemo and moving back from Las Vegas. Although she said she was coming to help with her grandkids, Shandell ended up being more of a burden than a blessing; and based on the cold shoulder that she felt from Kayla from time to time, she knew it.

Kayla didn't visit her mom as much as she should have. She resented her for the rough childhood that she endured living in one room with her all those years with no money, hand-me-down clothes, and shoes that were often falling apart at the sides or shredding underneath. Under her mother's supervision, Kayla became an excellent, albeit overweight cook, who hated washing dishes and doing laundry. She was a below-average student with no chance of going to college and began working at a fast-food restaurant as soon as she could get her working papers. Barely graduating with a diploma and having to pay half of the room's rent, when Kayla turned eighteen, she decided to leave Queens and live in a more functional household with her dad.

With her own room, a functional kitchen, and an unshared bathroom, she loved living in Brooklyn and would have stayed had it not been for the negative comments about her weight that she had to endure from her father. He wanted what was best for her but just didn't know how to express it. After seeing enough episodes of Georgia Housewives and Peaches, she decided that Atlanta would be a good place to try her hand and her luck. Kayla was unwavering about saving her money, which she was good at even though she didn't make much. She was already used to a minimalist lifestyle and did not pine over new shoes and fancy bags. She worked hard and stacked her checks, determined to go out and make it on her own.

Thanks to a helping hand from her mother, father, and grandmother, as well as the money she had saved, once she got to Atlanta, Kayla was able to rent a room and get a job at a popular roadside barbeque joint. It wasn't long after being in the city, "The A" as everyone called it, that she met Bobby. He was cute and charming and had a car, which made it easier for her to get to and from work. After getting pregnant, public housing and supplemental nutrition assistance benefits were easy to obtain, so she and Bobby moved in together, though he still maintained his room at his mother's house.

Kayla and Bobby had one son, then another, then another; and while Kayla attempted to maintain a job, it proved impossible with three pregnancies over six years. The last two years were even harder since the older boys' school attendance often rendered them sick. With no extra money for childcare, and Bobby always at the studio or sleeping, Kayla found herself staying home with sick children more often than going to work, which often resulted in resigning, quitting, or being fired. Although life was a struggle, Kayla loved her children and Bobby, and wouldn't have it any other way.

CHAPTER TEN

Paulo

PAULO PULLED UP TO THE HOUSE and opened his side of the garage just to find Marcella's car in his spot. Frustrated, annoyed, and overall tired from his day at work, he turned off the car and leaned his head back on the headrest. He closed his eyes and took a few deep breaths. He soon found himself dreaming about the summer before his senior year. He was polishing the floors one day at school when he ran into Mr. Vasquez.

"Mr. Vasquez," Paulo accosted him. "I'd like to talk to you about that Einstein internship. It's going to be important for me to get it next year to make sure that my family is good. My mother won't be able to take care of everything while I'm away at college and I just want to make sure that I leave her with as much as possible."

"That is understandable young man, and very commendable. Tell you what, come to my home on Marigold Street this afternoon when you are done here. It's the yellow house off of Pintar Avenue. I have some things you can help with in my workshop and on Saturday you can come back and clean out the pool. We can talk about the internship and make sure you have everything in place to secure your spot."

"Thank you so much," Paulo said. "I'll be there."

Paulo completed shining the floors at the school, all the while thinking that their principal had a pool. Paulo felt like he had hit the jackpot. With extra cash and the chance to solidify his entry into the internship, things were looking up.

Paulo was jolted awake by Marcella's horn. He restarted his car and backed up. She pulled her car out of the driveway and they met at each other's window.

"I'm running to the store for a bottle of wine and some whiskey," she said.

Paulo was sure it was for Nella and cringed at the thought of his wife being drunk again tonight. Paulo pulled into his spot and hurried in so that he could make dinner and play with Angel before it was time for him to go to bed. He didn't see Angel much anymore since Priscilla started working there. The house was clean, his clothes were ironed, and the dishes were washed and put away; all benefits of having a housekeeper. The problem was she almost doubled as a dad, so he spent very little time with Angel and didn't really see his son anymore. If things continued as they were, Nella wouldn't need him around at all; and that, he wouldn't tolerate.

CHAPTER ELEVEN

Priscilla

PRISCILLA ENJOYED WORKING WITH ANGEL. Aside from his daily outburst of not wanting to give up whoever's phone he was watching cartoons on as a bribe to eat his breakfast, he was mild-tempered. Priscilla had a growing suspicion that Angel had a speech impediment since he did not speak much and when he did, it sounded like gibberish. His parents chalked it up to his bilingual brain which was trying to make sense of both languages at the same time. They believed that he would grow out of the jibber-jabber once he could wrap his head around English or Spanish and would be able to make coherent sentences in the future.

Priscilla went about her daily chores quietly and efficiently. She mostly stayed out of Nella's way, which wasn't hard since Nella was always busy with clients. When she did have a moment of free time, Nella whisked herself away for a massage, a manicure, a wax, or a tanning session.

Occasionally, she had a gentleman caller come to the house for a midday shot of tequila or whiskey or rum. Nella didn't discriminate when it came to liquor or the time of day. Within the year that Priscilla had worked for them, she saw three different men visit Nella a handful of times.

There was Dr. Peterson, a tall, rugged, handsome white man with a full head of black hair dusted with streaks of gray. Nella introduced him as a colleague who was helping her with a difficult case. There was also Jonathan, an Afro-Cuban American who she knew from her college days and remained good friends with over the years. And then there was Antonio. Antonio was Marcella's ex-boyfriend. He was young compared to the two sisters; just twenty-five years old but very smart and very responsible. He had a good job working for a software company and often had business meetings in the area. When he did, he would swing by to take Nella to lunch if she was available or bring her food if she had clients. Nella did not mind making her clients wait while she ate with Antonio, often applying a fresh coat of lipstick before joining him in the kitchen.

Nella believed that Marcella should have married Antonio and secretly thought that her sister had made the biggest mistake of her life when she broke up with him. Although Marcella focused on Antonio's age, then twenty-three; making him ten years her junior, Nella argued that he was more responsible and more mature than anyone else Marcella had dated, including her last two husbands. Nella remained close friends with Antonio, claiming that she saw him as a little brother and wished that he had become part of the family.

Priscilla was often the one to open the door and fetch Nella for the arriving company but she knew never to ask for more information than Nella offered, to make herself invisible, and to never bring it up again. Interestingly enough, Nella never brought up her daytime company again either, not to Priscilla, not to Paulo, and not to Marcella.

Priscilla was surprised when the bell rang that evening. It was around the time that both Paulo and Marcella would be getting home, so she wasn't sure why they hadn't just come in through the garage. She opened the door to an attractive, albeit greasy-looking man of dark olive complexion, mid-height, and with the beginnings of a beer belly. Taken a little off guard, she inquired, "Can I help you?"

"Yes, is Marcella here?"

"She is not in at the moment."

"I'm Eugene, her boyfriend. She is expecting me."

"One moment, let me get the woman of the house," Priscilla closed the door and scurried to the other side of the house to find Nella. "There is a man here who says he's Marcella's boyfriend."

"Oh really? Where is he now?"

"He's outside."

"Is his name Eugene?"

"Yes."

"Let him in. I will be there shortly." Angel sat on her king-sized bed watching cartoons on the flat-screen television that was mounted high on the wall in the bedroom.

Priscilla opened the door for Eugene and invited him in. "Cup of coffee, water, juice, or tea?"

"No thanks pretty lady, we are going out to eat. Do you want to come?"

"Oh no, thank you."

As Nella approached the living room, Priscilla slowly excused herself and backed away to her bedroom. She retreated as Nella and Eugene formally introduced themselves to each other. Priscilla watched as Nella began to blush under Eugene's seductive stare and met his provocative talk with flirty speech and movements of her own. Confused but disinterested, Priscilla went to relax in her room. With the prospect of everyone going out to eat, there was nothing left for her to do and she would be able to enjoy the peace and quiet of an empty house for the evening. Priscilla laid back on her bed. She thought about calling Milagro to check up on her and see how she was doing in school. The last thing she heard was the motor on the garage door as either Marcella or Paulo pulled in. She fell into a deep sleep and didn't hear when the party of five left the house for dinner or when they returned.

CHAPTER TWELVE

Shandell

"HOT TEA AND MERCY. Hot tea and Mercy," Shandell whispered to herself as she rocked back and forth in pain.

"What are you saying?" Kayla snapped as she peeked her head out from the kitchen. She was cutting up vegetables to make her mother a pot of soup. One of Kayla's sons was at the kitchen table doing his homework, while the other one sat on the floor watching television. Annoyed that there was nowhere to put the youngest one who had fallen asleep in the car on the way home from daycare, Kayla brought the car seat with the sleeping child in it into the house and sat it down next to the front door.

"I'm not talking to you," Shandell snapped back.

"Well, who the hell you talkin' to then?"

"Leave me alone, Kayla."

"Leave you alone. Leave you alone. You got it. Let's go boys." Kayla put the knife down and left all of the vegetables on the counter and cutting board. She turned off the fire that was under the large pot of water and started to gather her stuff. "Get your stuff, let's go."

"Kayla, where are you going?"

"You told me to leave you alone, so I am. I'm leaving."

"What about the soup?"

"What about it?"

"What am I going to eat for dinner?"

"I'll send Jayden over with a plate of food for you after I finish cooking at my house."

"You know I can't eat what you make."

"You don't even know what it's going to be."

"Well, what are you making?"

"You'll just have to wait and see." With that, Kayla clicked the unlock button on the car fob and the boys opened the door and got in. She hoisted the car seat up and into the car, not bothering to buckle it in since they were only driving across the parking lot. She closed her mother's door, remembering not to lock it since she would send Jayden over later with food and didn't want him waiting outside for the twenty minutes that it often took Shandell to get out of bed and make it to the door.

"Hot tea and Mercy, please, just give me hot tea and Mercy," Shandell cried. Her cries became whimpers and finally, she fell asleep; the only time she truly felt relieved of the pain she was feeling. This time, though, she wasn't sure if she was crying because of the pain she felt in the tumors or the pain she felt in her heart.

CHAPTER THIRTEEN

Nella & Marcella

THE PARTY OF FOUR ADULTS and one child arrived at the well-known and very pricey seafood restaurant around seven. Marcella was beaming proudly over her beau. The twinkle in her eye when she spoke about him and the slight tilt of her head as she hung onto every one of Eugene's words displayed how into him she was. It was difficult for her to eat her meal in the time she spent fawning over him.

"You are glowing, Marcella. You must really be in love this time," Paulo said somewhat sarcastically.

Marcella rolled her eyes and Nella gave him a sharp look. He raised his glass to indicate to the waiter that he would indeed appreciate another beer. Marcella could hardly sit still. She was full of joy and excitement and could not wait until dessert, as she had planned, to share the good news with everyone. Nella already knew, but it would be a surprise to both Paulo and Eugene.

"So you are a construction worker, Eugene?"

"Aye, Paulo. Why are you questioning the man?" Nella blurted out, exasperated.

"What? All I did was ask him a question. I can't make conversation?"

"It's no problem. Yeah, my brother and I have a little construction company. It's not fancy and I'm not an architect or anything, but I get by."

"That's great. Very fascinating work," Nella said, smiling at him.

"Fascinating Nella, really?" Paulo was disgusted by Nella's compulsive need to be liked. He looked down at her chest and saw that her two top buttons were undone.

"I think it's fascinating."

"I think your cleavage is fascinating."

Nella looked down and scoffed at Paulo. She buttoned one of the buttons so as not to blow her cover of unfettered undercover flirting. It wasn't that she liked Eugene, and of course, he was hands off. She just liked the attention. She craved it really and couldn't count on Paulo to shower her with anything but criticism and complaints.

"You know what else is fascinating?" Marcella seized the opportunity to share the good news that had been bursting inside of her all day. Everyone turned and looked at her. With the biggest smile on her face, she whispered, "That I'm pregnant."

Nella let out a small shriek and clapped her hands. The two men continued to stare at her in bewilderment. Paulo picked up his beer and drank so as not to say all of the nasty thoughts about her being irresponsible, probably not knowing who the father was, and needing to get out of his house and get her own place, that were running through his head. After about three sips, although he simply wanted to call her stupid, logic clicked in and he reached his hand across the table to Eugene.

"Congratulations, brother," his hand still extended as he waited for Eugene to grab it for a shake.

"Well, aren't you going to say anything," Marcella's smile was growing smaller and her look of excitement became one more of concern and confusion.

"Oh yes," Eugene regained his composure and shook Paulo's hand. "Thank you, brother, thank you. Marcella," he turned back to his girl-friend of only six months, who had just gotten divorced, and to who he had no real plans of marrying. "Marcella, my goodness, Dios Mio, how are you feeling?"

"I am happy. How are you?"

Eugene had a lot of questions for Marcella and needed to tell her how he truly felt about all of this happening so fast. He knew it was not the right time and did not want to embarrass her in front of her sister and brother-in-law.

"I am happy, too," he lied and leaned over to give her a hug and a kiss.

Marcella was elated. Nella was also very happy for her sister who didn't have any children even though she had been married twice before. Paulo asked for the check and decided that he would not say anything for the rest of the night.

"Wait, we didn't even have dessert," Marcella squealed.

"Let's get it to go. I am tired and want to go home," Paulo's mood had turned very sour.

"It's only eight-thirty," Nella retorted.

"If you all want to stay, that is fine. I will take a cab home. I am tired and not feeling so well. Maybe I had one too many beers."

"Oh yes, maybe," Nella agreed with the fact that three beers were quite a lot for Paulo who often drank a glass of wine with dinner and called it a night. "Okay, let us go."

"As a matter of fact, you guys stay and enjoy. I think I will just go home and relax. Do you want me to take Angel with me or have him stay here with you?"

"You can take him," Nella said with plans of going to the dance club already percolating in her mind.

Paulo took the bill that the waiter had placed on the table and lifted Angel out of the wooden high chair. "I will pay for dinner, you can just deal with dessert and the tip. Congratulations to the two of you again. Nella, I will see you when you get home."

With that, he paid the one-hundred-eighty-dollar tab with two hun-dred dollar bills and held on to the change for the cab driver. With Angel in tow, he left the restaurant, hailed a cab, and went home. Immediately, he changed his son into his pajamas and turned to the cartoon network for Angel to watch until he organically fell asleep. Paulo took a long, hot shower, brushed his teeth, and got into bed. He knew it would be hours before Nella came home and frankly he was grateful for the solitude. He seethed at the thought of having to have a conversation with her about designing a nine-month exit strategy for Marcella. He was determined that she would not have that baby while still living under his roof.

Paulo's head throbbed slightly as he lay in bed with the international news channel blasting in the background. He fell asleep pretty quickly and stayed that way, sleeping hard and sound until his alarm went off at seven in the morning. He didn't hear when Nella crept into the bed at three-thirty, sweaty, drunk, and giddy. He didn't even hear the tiny yelp she let out as she secretly pleased herself under the covers while she thought about Eugene.

CHAPTER FOURTEEN

MONDAY MORNING WAS UNEVENTFUL as Priscilla got Angel ready for school. Paulo made protein shakes with some added pineapple and papaya for himself and Nella, who was moving slow and sluggishly in the stupor of her morning hangover. She had spent the entire weekend drinking rum and getting to know Eugene better as she and Marcella hung out and fixed up the guest room to Marcella's liking, completely ignoring Paulo and giving him the responsibility of minding Angel.

Paulo quickly and quietly moved through the kitchen and hastily got ready for work. He was not happy with his wife's shenanigans but did not want to argue with her again. His disdain for Marcella's presence was growing, but he knew it was a losing battle to dispute it with her sister. He felt small in his home. He felt helpless and hopeless and it took him back to a place that he desperately tried to forget. It brought up feelings that he consciously and unconsciously repressed for so many years. A dark time in his life when he felt alone, vulnerable, and helpless. Paulo gave Nella a quick peck on her lips, bid her a good day, and hurriedly left the house for work.

For no particular reason, Paulo sped to work. Perhaps he was so mad at Nella that his foot smashed the gas without him even realizing it. Perhaps, he was trying to leave his past so far behind him that to get away he had to speed into the future. As he careened through a red light, he swiftly got pulled over by a police officer idly sitting at the intersection eating a breakfast doughnut. This began the domino effect of the very bad day that Paulo ended up having.

After spending fifteen minutes with the police officer on Craig Road, and receiving a ninety-dollar ticket for speeding and a ticket for one hundred and fifteen dollars for running the red light, Paulo slowly crept to work fearing that he might have another run-in with the law before he got there. Walking through the door twenty-five minutes late and in an utter frenzy, he was met by his supervisor who said nothing but looked at his watch furiously.

"Sorry, I got pulled over."

"We had a nine o'clock with Zeron."

"Oh no, I completely forgot. How did it go?"

"It didn't. They left. We had nothing to show them without you there."

Paulo was the manager of a team of software technicians. He was multilingual, highly organized, and very meticulous. It was not hard for him to secure an entry-level position twelve years ago at the information technology, communications, and security company where he worked. Within just one year, he became a junior manager and two years later the manager of his own team. His job was to design advanced technology systems for large corporations, and he was very good at it.

After completing the Einstein scholarship program the summer after he graduated high school, where he worked hard to keep up with all of the other top math and science scholars of the country, he was offered an internship opportunity to study abroad with a leading French technology company. He remembered being torn between staying in Nicaragua to help his mother and traveling to France to intern for a year. The internship would house him and provide a small stipend while he lived and worked in Toulouse. He would receive training in fiberglass wire insulation, software upgrade, application design, various operating systems, and even space technology.

With the blessing of his mother, a school-sponsored airplane ticket to Europe, and the money he had managed to save, Paulo headed to France, where he lived and worked and became fluent in French. He loved everything about France: the fashion, the food, the wine, the women. He had worked extremely hard in high school and even harder during the internship, and he deserved to be there. It did not bother him that most of the other interns were from well-off families. He was smart and likable and fit in just fine. Paulo had resolved to make the best of the internship opportunity, especially since he had to work twice as hard for it, working as a janitor and doing odd jobs for his principal. Paulo gulped hard as he remembered those years and goosebumps formed on his arms. The hair on the back of his neck stood up.

After he finished the internship in Toulouse, the company asked him if he would be interested in being a Spanish translator at their Munich branch. Although he missed his family, he loved Europe and thought it would be a good idea to stay on the continent for as long as the opportunity would allow him to. With a full salary, he felt that he would be doing his family a disservice if he did not take the job. He agreed and moved to Germany, where he learned the language with ease and worked as a translator for two years. He was able to send much-needed money back to his family which helped his mother, who was aging quickly, a great deal, and financed the educational needs of his brothers and sisters. Paulo was also able to tour other European cities on weekends and national holidays. His favorite was Amsterdam, where he was able to satisfy some of his less agreeable vices. The hairs on his arm stood up and he began to feel the discomfort that sometimes crept into his psyche when he remembered those days from long ago. He gathered his attention back to his boss who was standing in front of him.

"I am so sorry. Has it been rescheduled?"

"No, it has not."

"I will call them, smooth it all over, and get them back in here. Or maybe even go there if it is more convenient."

"You better do something. That is a big contract and we cannot afford to lose it. That contract will pay for our entire department next year. If we don't get it, there's no telling what will happen."

Paulo's heart sank and a knot formed in his chest. For the third time in the last twenty-four hours, he felt the pressure of another man's authority on his back. He could feel the hot breath on his neck, the sweaty palms up his shirt, caressing his stomach and making their way to his back, slowly bending him over. Paulo began to feel sick. The contents of his morning breakfast gurgled in his stomach as the suppressed memories of his senior year of high school surfaced. Eugene, Officer Bettis, and now his boss, Matthew. He felt small, vulnerable, almost helpless.

"I will work it out," Paulo's voice cracked as he choked the words out of his throat and moved past Matthew, sweat beads glistening on his forehead and wetness forming under his arms.

Paulo somehow made it through the day, shuffling around meetings with his team and indeed securing another meeting with Zeron for the following Monday. At five-thirty, Paulo stumbled over his feet as he left the office, completely drained and in need of… He wasn't sure. He was feeling empty inside and in need of… He got into his car and began driving. Unwillingly, unknowingly, unbelievably, he found himself ambling down the Freezone area of Las Vegas. His throat closing, his head throbbing, his eyes narrowing, Paulo pulled off of the main street and into a parking spot on a lighted but empty block. He ran into a corner store for a bottle of water, opened it before he paid, drank it as he handed two one-dollar bills to the cashier, and exited the store, feeling only slightly better.

As he made his way back to his car, he heard a faint whistle piercing the wind from across the street. As he looked up, he saw exactly what he was looking for. Paulo motioned and the young prostitute jogged across the street.

"How old are you?" Paulo asked.

"Twenty-one."

Get in," Paulo instructed, and the young man did as Paulo said.

CHAPTER
FIFTEEN

〜〜〜

"HELLO DOCTOR, THIS IS DIANE WRIGHT, Shandell Wright's mother. I believe Shandell had you as a doctor when she lived here with me in Las Vegas. She wanted to get in touch with you because the cancer has come back and if you would please call me back, that would be very helpful." Shandell's mom left her phone number on the machine of the doctor whose card she found in the shoebox of trinkets that Shandell had left behind.

Mrs. Wright was very upset with Shandell and all of the decisions she had made over the years and most recently her decision to leave Las Vegas and go back to Atlanta. She felt that every decision that Shandell made was to get back at her. It seemed to her that every decision Shandell made wreaked havoc in Shandell's life and cost her money to clean up the mess.

Mrs. Wright never apologized to Shandell for taking her first-born baby boy away from her. She didn't think she had done anything wrong.

She thought she was saving Shandell from becoming a teenage pregnancy statistic. She thought she was giving that baby, her grandson, a fighting chance at success. She never explained it to Shandell though. From Shandell's point of view, her mother thought she wasn't capable of taking care of a baby and so gave her no choice, no option, showed her no respect, no love.

When Shandell finally found out that the lymph node protruding from her anus was not a hemorrhoid but instead a tumor, Mrs. Wright begged her to get the chemotherapy that the doctors had suggested. Shandell was still living in Queens, working as a paraprofessional during the day and waitressing at a diner in the evenings. Shandell was scared when she heard the word cancer and with Medicaid for health insurance, she did not think the doctors would give her the type of treatment necessary to keep her alive. Mrs. Wright remembered Shandell asking for her to help pay the fees for a private cancer treatment center. She had declined, telling her to use her county medical to get the treatment.

Instead of taking her mother's advice, Shandell decided to take matters into her own hands and follow a more holistic approach to her treatment. It was a good plan and would have worked if she had the money and support. With no extra funds and Medicaid not covering herbs, tinctures, acupuncture, acupressure, reflexology, detoxes, cleanses, and photon radiation, Shandell was stuck doing the bare minimum; juicing antioxidant-rich fruits and vegetables, eating apricot seeds, and indulging in daily sitz baths. It was helpful but it wasn't enough. Cancer spread into her colon and metastasized to a point where it hurt to defecate.

Shandell moved to Atlanta to live with Kayla who couldn't handle having her mother live there at her house. Already stressed with her three children and a failing relationship, after two weeks, Shandell's nighttime whimpers and daily demands became too much. Mrs. Wright remembered when Shandell called her sobbing over the phone to tell her that Kayla had asked her to leave.

"How could she kick me out at a time like this? She doesn't love me. No one loves me."

"Oh honey, she loves you. We all love you. But you need to go on and get that chemo so that you can get better."

"Ma, please let me do this my way. Please!"

Mrs. Wright did not know what to do or say to make Shandell undergo the chemotherapy. She wanted to yell at her. Scream some sense into her. Ask her why she was making a dumb decision just to hurt her mother. Instead, she found a compassion that she rarely used with her daughter and said, "Why don't you come and stay out here with me for a while?"

With nowhere to go and very little ability to be independent, Shandell agreed. She didn't think it was a good idea, but the truth was, it was the only idea. Her mother bought the plane ticket for the following week and with one checked luggage, one carry on, and a doughnut ring to sit on, Shandell boarded a flight to Las Vegas to go and live in her mother's five-bedroom, three-bathroom, ranch-style house with a living room, dining room, sitting room, parlor, office, jacuzzi-style bathtub, and pool; the spoils of a settlement she received from a slip and fall in a New York City building twenty years prior. No longer able to work and with plenty of money in the bank, she moved to Nevada.

Shandell spent every moment of the plane ride dreading the fact that she would be living with her mother. She cringed at the arguments she imagined they would have; the discomfort she would be in; the bland food that her mother would reluctantly make. Shandell was miserable about the whole situation and when she landed in Vegas, could barely muster a smile and a hug for her mother, who picked her up in a gold Jaguar.

Mrs. Wright chalked up Shandell's bad mood to the cancer and an uncomfortable flight. She did not realize that the tumor Shandell was harboring in her rectum was from years of pent-up anger and frustration at her mother, a literal pain in the ass. She had held in so much of what she was feeling over the years, swallowed so much anger and pain that it was finally expressing itself as a fungating lesion, similar to their relationship. Shandell could no longer hold it in or hold it together. She was now face-to-face with her mother, who she had ignored, run from, and secretly disdained for so many years. She had an opportunity to make things right and begin to heal or to continue to cover up the wounds and scars that Mrs. Wright had left her with.

Shandell was in Vegas, at her mother's house, ready to heal. She had Kayla ship her juicer in the mail and had signed up for a farm-fresh weekly box of organic fruits and vegetables. She had big plans of using the jacuzzi for some water protocols that included Epsom salt, sea salt, apple cider vinegar, and cannabidiol bath bombs. She was going to maintain a completely vegetarian diet and she had found a company in Colorado that was willing to ship her THC oil that she could take orally. Shandell was feeling very optimistic. She felt that if she could keep the arguments with her mother to a minimum then she was in the right environment to rest, rejuvenate, and allow her body to restore itself from the inside out. She was ready to heal. What she didn't know was that her mother had already booked an appointment for her with an oncologist, first thing the next morning.

CHAPTER SIXTEEN

~~~~

PRISCILLA WAS STANDING OVER the ironing board, sweating as she ironed Paulo's long-sleeved, collared shirts. Las Vegas is hot, she thought, why would anyone need to wear long-sleeves? Just then, her phone rang. It was her daughter.

"Milagro, hello, hi, how are you?

"I'm fine, mommy, how are you?"

"I'm fine. How is school?"

"It is fine too. I have finals this week and next and then I have to leave the school."

"Leave, why?"

"Because classes are over until the next semester and everyone has to evacuate the dorms. We can come back the last week of August."

"June, July, August, that's three months. Where are you supposed to go for three months?"

"I don't know mommy, that's the way college works."

"Well, why didn't someone tell me?"

"Where is everyone else going?"

"Home."

"Aye, Dios, Mio. Okay, you have three weeks, you said?"

"I have to be out by the 27th at the latest."

"Okay, I will talk to my boss and see if you can come and stay here with me for the summer. Don't worry about it. But, how are you, mi amor, ¿Estas bien?"

"Yes, I am fine mommy, thanks. Just have to study for these tests."

"You study. You will do well. You are a smart girl. I know you will do well. Do you need anything?"

"I am fine. I just need to know what to do once school is over, you know, like where to go."

"I know, I know. I understand. I will work it out and let you know. Don't worry about anything except passing your tests, okay?"

"Okay mommy, thank you. I love you."

"I love you too, hija. I will talk to you later. Call me this weekend when you are free."

"Okay, I will. Bye."

"Bye-bye."

Priscilla was sweating even more now though she hadn't been ironing for the entire conversation. Although she dreaded the conversation that she would have to have with Nella, she decided that she would not stress about it. Nella was reasonable most of the time and it would only be three months. It was her daughter, for heaven's sake; Nella would understand, right? Priscilla sure hoped she would.

CHAPTER SEVENTEEN

~~~~~

"IF IT WEREN'T FOR YOU believing in me and forcing me to have the confidence to believe in myself, I wouldn't have been able to accomplish this. I swear. You are the best, Dr. Merced."

"Please call me Nella," Nella peered over her glasses at the client on the couch.

"Dr. Nella. I do not know what I would have done without you. I walked in there with my back straight and head held high and told them that I was the right man for the job. I even bought a new suit and had my shoes shined before I got there. Man, I tell you. I have health insurance and dental and a 401K. A 401K."

"I could not be happier for you," Nella smiled.

"And my mother is so proud of me."

"The mother whom you live with, right?"

"Yes."

"Do you plan to move out?"

"Move out, why?"

"Well because you're thirty-six and have never lived on your own."

"But my mother needs me."

"Does she?"

"Yes, I think she…"

"Has she told you that she needs you?"

"Well, she doesn't have to. I know."

"How do you know?"

"Because if I wasn't there, who would take the garbage?"

"How old is your mother?"

"She is like, fifty-nine or sixty."

"Can she walk?"

"Yes."

"Does she work?"

"Yes, says she'll retire in a few years."

"Do you pay the rent?"

"No."

"Any bills?"

"Not really. I give her two hundred dollars a month."

"For what? Food?"

"For whatever she uses it for."

"Do you shop for groceries?"

"She does that."

"Do you cook?"

"She does that."

"Do you eat?"

"Of course, Dr. Nella, what's with all of the questions?"

"I am going to tell you the same thing that I told you when you thought you couldn't get a job, Jim. You are stronger than you think. You do not need to live with your mother to succeed. You will be alright if you live on your own, independently. You, my dear, just have to believe in yourself and have the confidence to move forward with bold courage. You can and will find a way to live without your mommy. You just have to have faith and rely on your talents, abilities, interests, and experiences. She will still be there, but you have to live your own life and allow her the pleasure of living hers. She already took care of you and when she needs you to take care of her, really needs you to take care of her, you can move back or move her in with you, but right now, the key is knowing that you are a strong, independent man who can and will make it by himself without mom." Dr. Nella allowed a long pause to idle in the air so that her words could sink into the head, heart, and spirit of her client. "Jim, are you okay?"

"Yes, Dr. Nella, thank you. I have a lot to think about."

"That is the best way to use these sessions. Think about it. Spend the week contemplating and coming up with the best choices for yourself."

"I'll do that."

"Very good, Jim. Good. That concludes our session for today. Shall I schedule you for the same time next week?"

"Yes, please. Thank you, Dr. Nella, thank you."

"You're welcome," Nella said as Jim left the office. "Aye, gringos." It always baffled her how lost and confused people who seemed like they should have it all together were. With all the privilege, all the education, and all of the money that was available to so many others in the country, they still wandered through life clueless.

Lost in her thoughts, Nella was jolted to attention by the sound of the buzzer. She had a new client scheduled, and she was right on time.

"Hello, I am Joan Patel, and you must be Dr. Merced, is it?"

"Hi Joan, welcome. Come in, sit down. You can call me Dr. Nella."

"Dr. Nella, nice to meet you. Thank you for agreeing to see me."

"No problem. Now, tell me why you are here. What makes you want to come and see a shrink like me?"

"A shrink, that's funny," Joan quipped back at Nella who was indeed being cheeky. Joan was of Asian descent, but Nella couldn't figure out if she was Filipino, Vietnamese, or from some other eastern country. She was dressed in a flattering blue dress from a famous woman designer, a black blazer which she took off before sitting down, black pumps, and a large black purse that looked like it had seen better days. "Well, I'm a teacher."

"What grade?"

"Sixth."

"How many years?" Nella uncharacteristically interrupted her client to ask trivial questions.

"Nine years," Joan waited to see if Nella had any other inquiries.

"Go on," Nella broke the silence and encouraged Joan to continue.

"I'm leaving the profession at the end of this school year to become a full-time housewife. I am originally from Minnesota but moved here three years ago after I met my husband. Well, he wasn't my husband then, but we met and got married the following year. Well, I moved here to be with him and then we got married and it seems that I may have made a mistake."

"Moving here or getting married?"

"Both."

"How long had you known him before you moved?"

"Three months."

"And then you got married, when?"

"Six months later."

"You moved from Minnesota."

"Yes."

"Where did you meet him?"

"At an airport. We were waiting at the same gate to get on a flight. I was on my way from Vegas back to Minneapolis after my grandmother's funeral and had a connection in Charlotte. He was flying to visit his parents. We were on the same flight. He spoke to me at the gate and then swapped seats with someone to sit next to me. The rest is kind of history."

"The rest is history? No, my dear, there is more between Las Vegas and North Carolina, much more between Minnesota and your Las Vegas move, even more between your Las Vegas move and your Las Vegas marriage, and so much more between you saying yes and ending up in my office. How long have you been married now?"

"Two years."

"And he's from here?"

"No. He lives here but is from Pennsylvania originally. He has been living here for the last two years."

"How old are you, Joan?"

"Thirty-five."

"And your husband?"

"Forty-five."

"And you are going to quit teaching, you said?"

"Yes."

"To become a housewife?"

"Yes."

"His idea or yours?"

"His."

"Do you have a say in the matter?"

"It is easier if I stop working."

"He supports you?"

"Yes. Pays all of the bills and gives me money."

"Like an allowance."

"Well, something like that."

"He doesn't like you working?"

"He likes being able to take care of me."

"Why is that?"

"It's the old-fashioned man in him. His dad took care of his mom, and he wants to do the same for me."

"Does he have any children?"

"No."

"Does he want any?"

"Yes, right away."

"Telling. Why doesn't he want you working, again?"

"He likes being able to take care of me. Telling people he takes care of me."

"Is that the only reason?"

"Yes."

"Have you asked him?"

"No, not really. It's what he said when he asked me to stop and I believe him."

"How long ago did he ask you?"

"At the beginning of this year, right before I went back to work after the holiday break."

"Did anything happen over the holiday break that might have made him want you to quit?"

"No."

"It was a good holiday?"

"Yes."

"Did you get lots of gifts?"

"Oh yes," Joan smiled and clasped her hands together. "My husband bought me everything I asked for. And a few parents gave me little trinkets, like a scarf, gloves, candles, and books. Oh, and my principal gave me a beautiful crystal vase."

"For flowers?"

"Uh-huh."

"Is your principal a man or a woman?"

"A man."

"Did he give everyone a gift?"

"I don't know."

"Has he ever given you a gift before?"

"Well, this is my first year teaching at the school, so no, it is the first gift he has given me."

"Does he like you?"

"Heavens no, not like that."

"Does he flirt with you?"

"No, not really."

"Hmmm. Telling," Nella let the silence sit in the air for a little while, and just when Joan began to shift her weight on the couch said, "Joan, I am glad you are here. There is some work to be done, on your marriage and yourself. Our time is up for today but I would love to see you at your earliest convenience."

"This time next week works for me."

"Good."

Joan got up and left. Nella sat back to take a moment to breathe. When she decided to get up, she went back into the house, into the kitchen, straight to the liquor cabinet, and poured herself a rum and coke to chase her shot of whiskey. Nella went to the living room to sit down for a moment and put her feet up. Just then, Priscilla entered the room. Shocked to see Nella, she thought it was a good time to bring up the conversation she had been dreading since her daughter told her about college closing in a few weeks.

"Ms. Nella, can I talk to you for a moment?"

"Is everything alright? Did something happen to Angel?" Nella briefly became concerned thinking that something had happened to her son.

"Yes, everything is okay. Angel is fine. I'm going to pick him up from school shortly."

"Okay, good. What is it then? I cannot give you a raise right now."

"Oh no, I wasn't asking for a raise. I am happy with everything."

"Okay, good. What is it then?" Nella was starting to become impatient.

"My daughter just finished her first year of college and she, well, she lives on campus, but the dorms get closed down at the end of the school year, so she has to leave the school until classes start back in August. She doesn't have anywhere to go and so I wondered if she could stay here with me for the summer. She won't be a problem. I'll buy her food separately and she will just stay in my room. Maybe she'll get a job so she wouldn't even be here during the day, just the evenings, you know. Would it be alright?" Priscilla nervously blurted out everything all at once.

"Aye, no, I don't think so. Her being here might take your attention away from your duties and Angel. And also, Marcella just moved in so there are four adults living here. I just don't think it is a good idea for now, sorry."

"Oh, oh wow, I didn't expect that; I'm not sure what I'll do with Milagro for the summer."

"Things always work themselves out for the best," Nella said in a kind and reassuring tone. She finished her drink, looked at her watch, and began to get up.

"It's time to get Angel, no?"

Priscilla looked at the clock on the wall. "Yes, I'm leaving now."

Both women departed, walking separate ways; Nella back to her office with her mind on nothing in particular, and Priscilla out the front door with thoughts of her daughter heavy on her heart.

Over a dinner of pork chops, mashed potatoes, and green beans, Paulo's disgust towards Marcella was palpable. He passive-aggressively showed his disdain by not passing her the bowl of potatoes, not including her in the conversation that he made with Nella, and even not answering Marcella when she asked how his day was.

"Paulo, I think you are being rude to Marcella," Nella finally said after she and her sister exchanged glances of confusion for the third time.

"Rude. In my house? No, I don't think so."

"Well, you are completely ignoring her when she speaks to you."

"Marcella," Paulo turned his attention directly to her, "You can't stay here until the baby comes. You have to be gone before you have it. I don't know what you and Eugene are planning but he needs to take you in and take care of you and that child."

"You aren't my father, Paulo."

"But this is my house. You are not cooperative and you just, you just, you just can't stay here past nine months."

"Nella?!?!" Marcella turned to her sister for support in a half yell, half question.

Nella was quietly glaring at Paulo. Everyone was staring at her. She didn't speak. She held her hand up to Marcella and then turned to her sister. "No te preocupes hermana," she said and then turned back to her plate of food.

"Don't worry? What does that mean, don't worry?" Paulo questioned Nella's words to her sister.

"It means don't worry. She can stay here as long as she wants. Even after she has the baby."

"Nella," Paulo was incredulous.

"Priscilla," Nella uncharacteristically yelled from the kitchen table. "Priscilla, please come here."

Priscilla was on her knees at the side of her bed holding her Rosary and praying when she was jolted to reality at the sound of hearing her name. She got up slowly and placed the Rosary in the drawer of the nightstand next to her bed.

"Priscilla, ven aca," Nella yelled once more as Priscilla emerged from her room. She made her way to the kitchen and stood quietly next to

Nella awaiting the request from her boss, who Priscilla wasn't all that keen on hearing from at this time.

"Priscilla needs for her daughter to stay with her this summer between semesters of college," Nella spoke into the air without looking directly at anyone, "Isn't that right, Priscilla?"

"Yes, ma'am."

"So, she can stay with you in your room. She has full access to the house, as you do, but she must clean up after herself and not make too much noise as teenagers sometimes do with their music and friends. Oh, no company."

"Nella," Paulo said in a whisper as he put his head down.

"Thank you so much, Mrs. Nella. Thank you so much."

"That is all, Priscilla."

Priscilla skipped back to her room to call her daughter with the good news. She was so happy, she was almost crying. As she grabbed her cell phone off the nightstand, she opened the drawer, pulled out the Rosary, and kissed it.

"Nella," Paulo said, "We do not need another person in this house." Nella was silent. "You are just doing this to be spiteful."

"I can say the same for you," she said as she got up from the table and walked toward her bedroom, not saying another word and not looking back; not even for Angel who sat in his highchair with mashed potatoes on his face.

Paulo looked at Marcella who grabbed her plate, got up, and went to her room to finish her dinner. He placed his hands over his face and then slowly got up to begin his nightly task of putting the food away and cleaning up the kitchen.

"Da-Da," Angel said.

Paulo began to cry.

HOT TEA & MERCY

CHAPTER EIGHTEEN

Kayla

"GRANDMA, I DON'T KNOW what we are going to do," Kayla sat at her kitchen table with her forehead resting in her hand as she spoke into the telephone.

"Well, I don't know either, honey. She was just fine when she left here. What happened?"

"I don't know. She said she was eating a vegetarian diet, but something about nutritional yeast made it grow. It just came back. Everything came back."

"She was supposed to get that last round of chemo, you know?"

"Yeah, but she didn't like having that portal sticking out of her chest."

"That is how they administered the medicine."

"She felt open. It was right to her heart."

"Well, look at her now."

"She is in a lot of pain. She cries every day. She can hardly walk."

"Oh no, oh honey."

"Grandma, I cannot take care of her. It's hard seeing her like this and I can't keep going over there every day."

"She's just across the street."

"Yeah but I have these boys and my own life. You have to do something."

"Okay, I'll come down there. Hold tight while I check flights and everything. Give me about a week or two."

"Two?" Kayla yelled into the phone, "You better make it one."

"I'll do my best. I love you, honey, bye." Mrs. Wright hung up the phone dreading the idea of taking a five-hour plane ride from Las Vegas to Atlanta. At seventy-three years old, she was still spry, but travel took a lot out of her. It would be even more taxing to visit her daughter who looked, as Kayla explained, like she was dying.

Mrs. Wright logged in to the computer and searched the inexpensive flight website for a direct flight as soon as possible. She found a one-way ticket for just over two hundred dollars departing in six days. She decided that was reasonable and figured she would book the flight back after she got to Atlanta and assessed the situation. Would she stay? Would she bring Shandell back with her? She wasn't sure. At that moment, she realized that the doctor she had left a message for had not called her back.

"Oh dear," she said out loud to no one, "Where did I put that card?" Mrs. Wright got up to look for it but got sidetracked when she decided to get a glass of water. Afterward, she busied herself with doing the dishes and before long she was making dinner. She was in bed watching the late show when it crossed her mind again. "Oh shoot," she said out loud to no one, realizing that she hadn't found the card, much less called the doctor that Shandell so desperately requested. Mrs. Wright resigned to remember to do it in the morning, turned off the television, and went to sleep.

CHAPTER NINETEEN

Joan & Simone

"HOW WAS THE THERAPIST," Simone asked her sister as Joan walked through the front door.

"I'm not sure. She was good, I think. I don't know. It was just the first time."

"Well, what did y'all talk about?"

"Nothing that deep. My job, my marriage."

"Your marriage, well that is pretty deep."

"Nothing deep about it. Just that I got married pretty quickly and now I am a wife."

"Do you regret getting married?"

"No, not really, but I just didn't think that there would be all of these changes."

"Like what, moving to Vegas?"

"I knew I was going to move, but like, like; like having to quit my job."

"Yeah, but now you get to be a housewife. You can do nothing in this big, beautiful house all day long."

"I don't want to do nothing all day. Not to mention, being a housewife is not even easy. There are so many things to do around the house."

"I would love to be a housewife. Netflix and chill."

Joan didn't even know that she was shaking her head from side to side until her sister said, "What?"

"What?"

"What are you shaking your head at? So many women would love to be in your position. Big house. Nice car. A handsome husband who spoils you and tells you that you don't have to work. Ungrateful."

"He didn't tell me that I don't have to work. He told me that he doesn't want me to work. There is a difference. And I'm not ungrateful at all."

"What's the difference? No work is no work."

"Speaking of no work, when do you plan to get a job?" Joan was annoyed with Simone who called her ungrateful.

"Humph."

"Oh, that's it? The conversation is over?"

"I'm looking, but not everyone got to go to college, so it isn't as easy for me to find a job as it is for some people."

"If by some people you mean me, we grew up in the same household with the same opportunities."

"But you were ma's favorite."

"You just didn't want to go to school."

"I didn't like school."

"Well say that. Don't blame me or ma or anyone else."

"I'm saying."

"What are you saying?"

"I'm looking for something. There are these job search apps that I'm on every day, so something will come up."

"And if something doesn't?"

"Dang, shorty, you want me gone that bad, I just got here."

"Why did you come to Vegas anyway?"

"To start over. To enjoy the sun. To meet a rich man at the high rollers table."

"To start over from what?"

"Well, you know me and Lou broke up and I just couldn't afford that apartment by myself."

"Why didn't you go back home?"

"With ma? Please, we do not get along."

"She is your mother."

"Yeah, a mother fu,"

"Don't say it, don't you say it."

"You are her baby girl. I am nothing."

Joan started shaking her head again, this time consciously. Simone had blamed their mom for everything that had gone wrong in her life. They had each done wrong towards each other over the years, but their mom was forgiving, Simone was not and disdained her.

"Not to mention, it's cold in the Midwest, baby. I needed a little sunshine in my life."

"You're the oldest, the firstborn, so that is something. And when you asked if you could come to visit, you did not say it was long-term."

"And it won't be. Give me a few months and I'll be on my feet and out of your hair."

"I love you, but please make it shorter than three months. I am newly married and trying to figure things out around here with my new husband."

"Well, when you need me to leave, just tell me and I'll go live in my car."

"Simone, you know we would not have you living in your car. Just, make yourself comfortable yet invisible."

"You won't even know I'm here, sis."

CHAPTER TWENTY

Simone

ALTHOUGH YOU COULD TELL that Simone and Joan were sisters, they each had very distinct features that set them apart and made them unique, what many would call exotic. With Asian-Indian blood, they each had long, jet black, silky hair. Simone's hair was a little thicker than Joan's, making it fuller but less manageable. Each of the ladies had clear, smooth skin. Simone was pecan-colored, and Joan was almond-complected. When they were young, Simone's lighter skin gave her one-up on her sister, but as they got older, Joan's darker skin made her more alluring.

In their teenage years, Joan was a skinny bag of bones, while Simone had a lot more meat on her. Her thickness was a hit with all of the neighborhood boys. As the two aged past their twenties and into their thirties, Joan filled out nicely and Simone got fat. Though both women were pretty, Joan carried herself with more confidence because she was proud of her body and happy with the way she looked. Simone had an odd relationship with food that became stranger to Joan each day as her sister would say she was vegetarian while eating fast-food fried chicken, or say she was on a diet while hiding bags of potato chips, sacks of cookies, and a box of doughnuts in her car or behind the bedroom curtains.

Even with her lack of confidence, Simone still received a lot of attention from men who loved long-haired, light-skinned, pretty girls with big butts; and there were a lot of them. Unfortunately, most didn't stick around for too long after getting to know her. With a bad attitude and a propensity to give it up too soon, princess Simone often found herself meeting a guy, going on three dates with him, having sex, and then wondering why he wasn't calling back. This didn't help her self-esteem and over the years, she became angrier and angrier at love, life, and Joan, who seemed to have it all.

Simone seemed to be caught red-handed as the garage door opened and the light automatically came on. The house was quiet and it was a little after midnight when she decided that since she couldn't sleep, it would make sense to sneak in a joint. She didn't know if there were any rules about smoking in the house and she didn't want to anger her sister. So there she was standing in the middle of the garage puffing on a doobie when it drove Viraj. Simone stepped to the side while he pulled in. She put the joint out and tried to wave the smoke out of the air. Viraj stepped out of the car once it was in park and the ignition was turned off.

"You smoke?"

"Yeah, seems that way," Simone laughed.

"What you smokin'?"

"Just some regular green," Simone answered.

"I have some better stuff than that. Come inside. What are you doing out here anyway?"

"I didn't want to bother Joan with the smoke." The two walked inside the side door that led to the kitchen.

"Joan ain't trippin' on that," Viraj pulled out a bag of marijuana from under the sink and took a little bit out. He patted his pockets to find the blunt wrapper that he had just bought at the corner gas station before coming home. Realizing that it was still in the car, he headed back out to the garage. "Break that up," he motioned to the weed.

Simone came around the kitchen counter and began to break up the weed that Viraj had left there. She looked at the bag he left behind and debated grabbing some out for herself then thought better of it. She looked in the bag just as she heard his car door slam. There was one good-sized nugget on top that she grabbed with her right hand as she closed the plastic bag down with her left. Viraj walked back in and held up the blunt.

"Got it," he said smiling.

From the Punjab region, Viraj was taller than most Indian men standing at six feet. He was café au lait colored, with straight black hair, and a salt-and-pepper sprinkled mustache that made him look about ten years older than the forty-five that he was. He started breaking down the blunt and as Simone moved back around to her seat at the counter, she said, "I'll be right back."

Simone ran upstairs to tuck the nugget away in the corner of her top dresser drawer after she wrapped it in facial tissue. As she came back down the hallway, the floor creaked, waking Joan up from the slumber that had already slightly been disturbed by the sound of the garage door. Viraj put the finishing touches on the blunt he rolled in Simone's absence just as she walked back into the kitchen. "Do you have a lighter?"

Simone took out the lighter that she had in her pajama pocket and handed it to him. He lit the blunt and began to smoke it. He was passing it to Simone just as Joan came down the stairs and rounded the corner into the living room where she could directly see the two sharing the smoke.

"Hey, I didn't know you were home," she said to Viraj as she walked over and kissed him. "Are you hungry?"

"I'm good. I got some fast food on the way in. How are you feeling?"

"I'm good, thanks, tired." Joan glanced at Simone who was sitting at the counter wearing a matching pajama set. "I have extra robes," she said to her sister. "Remind me to give you one tomorrow."

Joan sat in the kitchen with her husband and sister painfully trying to keep her head up and her eyes open. Simone could feel the tension growing in the air and so after a few more pulls, bid the two good night.

Viraj finished smoking the blunt and put out the roach in the ashtray. Joan got up and began to ascend the stairs as he poured himself a glass of juice. He came up shortly after her and got in the shower. Joan was asleep before he got into the bed.

CHAPTER TWENTY-ONE

Viraj

VIRAJ WAS A HANDSOME MAN, though it took him many years and a lot of money in the bank to believe that he was. Growing up as a middle child in an Indian family, he had an older brother that his father doted on and a younger sister who was the apple of his mother's eye, which left him to be the scapegoat for everything under the sun that went down in his childhood home.

His mother and father had been together since their early twenties. His father, a former surgeon, was stern and strict. His mother was a God-fearing, temple-attending Sikh, and always had been. She was also stern when it came to not sparing the rod, which Viraj got the most of.

Viraj grew up feeling ugly and like he didn't fit in. Never good in school, he clashed with his teachers daily and sometimes had fights with the other students. Growing up in a racist county just outside of

Pittsburgh, Pennsylvania, he was taught, both subtly and in blatant terms, that he was inferior because of his skin color.

When he turned eighteen, barely graduating high school, he decided to move to Philadelphia, where he heard brown people lived better lives and could operate more freely without being scrutinized by white people for everything that they did.

Viraj's father gifted him his old Audi and upgraded to something far fancier for himself. He also gave him a five-thousand-dollar loan that he really did not want or expect back to help his middle son get off to a decent start in his new city. Neither of them told Viraj's mom about the money and so she faithlessly expected him to be back home in three to six months.

Viraj was grateful for the gifts from his father but was not impressed. He had paid for Viraj's brother to attend a prestigious college in Pennsylvania, also to become a doctor, and his younger sister was two years away from finishing her private school education. Viraj had neither of those luxuries nor did he want them. He packed up the ten-year-old Audi with a few bags of clothes, shoes, some canned groceries from his mom's pantry, and nothing else. He stopped at Big Pat's preppy trap house on the East End of Pittsburgh in the Squirrel Hill district before leaving the city and dropped three thousand dollars of the money his dad gave him on two pounds of the best weed he could buy for that price. Camouflaging and securing it among the bags of clothing in his trunk, he carefully drove the four-hour drive to Philly where he rented an extended stay room and started his entrepreneurial venture as a drug dealer.

Cautious and clandestine, Viraj spoke very little and trusted no one. After breaking down the two pounds and doubling his money within three weeks, he made the trip back to Big Pat's. This became routine and more frequent as he got to know people and built up his clientele. After renting two hotel rooms, one for his home and one for his business, for eight months, and meticulously saving every penny that didn't go back into his venture or directly to his cost of everyday living, Viraj took the lease of a rent-to-own condominium in East Falls. With his sights on owning the condo and then eventually a house, Viraj kept his head down, worked hard, and stayed out of trouble.

Never wanting to stick out due to his somewhat low self-esteem, he was notorious for blending in. This made him almost invisible in clubs and at parties. He watched everything around him, almost unseen; and made seamless interstate runs twice a week. Within five years he owned the condo and ten years later he sold it for a pretty penny. He used some of the money for the down payment to a three-bedroom, two-bathroom home that he purchased, some of the money to upgrade his product from green to white, and placed the rest in a money market account to accrue a decent amount of interest each year.

He dabbled in real estate over the years, and though he lost some money from the first few deals he did, he later made a good amount of money once he partnered with an Armenian guy named Alik. Alik lived in Las Vegas and flew into Philly every month to attend auctions, check on his properties, and purchase foreclosures. Alik took a liking to Viraj and showed him the ins and outs of flipping houses for a profit. Viraj had visited Alik in Vegas a few times and liked the scene; he even thought about moving there once or twice over the years.

With age creeping up on his parents and the drug scene getting hot in Philadelphia, Viraj decided that he had had a good twenty-two year run and it was time to get out of the game and the city while he was still young and free. At the age of forty, with a few properties under his belt, plenty of money in the bank, and a clean record, he told his parents that he was planning to move to Nevada and asked them if they would like to go with him. His parents had a hearty laugh.

Viraj felt small and stupid, just as he had all those years growing up. Newly retired and with plenty of money in the bank himself, Viraj's dad had purchased a three-bedroom, ranch-style home on a few acres of land in Charlotte that he and his wife were planning to move to.

"Why didn't you tell me," Viraj asked as he sat in the living room of the house he grew up in.

"I didn't know I needed your permission," his dad said nonchalantly.

"You don't. But courtesy would dictate that you tell your kids that you are leaving the state."

"Your brother and sister know."

"Wow," Viraj was both shocked and hurt.

"Well, they come and see us or call more often than you do. That is why they know and you don't," Viraj's mom piped up seeing the hurt on her son's face.

"Oh sonny, you know it is getting too cold for our bones here. I can't be out there shoveling snow anymore. This was a long time coming. You should have known," his dad said, taking the responsibility off of himself and placing it on Viraj as he had done so often over the years.

"That's cool. Okay, well, I'm moving to Las Vegas at the end of the year. You are welcome to visit me anytime and if you give me your address in North Carolina, I will come to see you guys as often as I can."

With that, Viraj left his parents' home and made arrangements to move to Nevada. He sold all but one of his Philadelphia properties, placing most of the money in a bank account, and allocating some of it to the idea of a future home that he would purchase to stay in when he visited his folks in Charlotte.

Like all of Viraj's plans, this one went swimmingly well. He stayed with Alik for three months as he got to know his new city. He found a seven-bedroom, five-bathroom house with a three-car garage, a large front yard, and a nice-sized backyard that was available at a short-sale price. Using the knowledge that he acquired about real estate over the years, he worked his magic, and the house was his. He was happy with his purchase and felt proud of himself. He wished his parents would come and visit him one day so that they could be proud of him too; so that they could realize how smart he actually was. Deep down, he knew they would never come, and even further down, he knew that they would never truly be proud of him. Though no one ever brought it up, everyone had their suspicions about how he made his money. His mother secretly disdained it. His siblings were jealous that he had more than them even after all of those years of college. Viraj truly was unsure of what his father thought, but if he had to guess, it was that his dad didn't even like him.

Twenty-five years after leaving his family home in Pittsburgh, and two years after leaving Philadelphia, Viraj was ready to settle down, get married, and legitimize his entire life; or so he thought. As organized, thoughtful, and meticulous as he did everything else, he found a beautiful, smart woman who did everything by the books. She had a college degree

and worked as a middle school history teacher. With a good amount
of money in the bank and a thousand dollars coming in monthly from
his Philly rental property, Viraj didn't need to sell drugs anymore. His
mortgage was easily covered, and he lived meagerly. He was an average
guy aside from his mini-mansion and the extravagant automobile that he
decided to purchase for his forty-fifth birthday.

The cost of their small wedding was a drop in the bucket; however,
it did put a slight dent in his bank account. Coupled with his new wife's
spending habits, which were a little unorthodox for his tastes, he began
thinking of ways to have more income. Joan liked to visit her family in
Minneapolis quite often which cost a pretty penny over the previous year.
She was also used to taking trips with her girlfriends during the summer
months when she was not teaching. Not only did those trips not cease,
but she added another one for her and him. Monthly trips to the spa for
her hair and nail appointments, as well as weekly massages also began
adding up. It didn't help that Viraj liked to buy expensive clothing from
the Fashion Mall for his wife. He couldn't help that he wanted to dress
her up so she looked good all of the time. She was his wife, his trophy.

To make matters worse, he almost demanded that she stop working
after he noticed that her boss was giving her more attention than ap-
propriate. Viraj wasn't necessarily jealous. He had always wanted to give
the woman he married the option to stay home and raise children, as
his father did for his mother. He had planned to get Joan pregnant soon
enough and it would have been a natural progression out of the working
world and into the home, but after he saw the extravagant Christmas
gift Joan received from her principal, Viraj immediately asked her to stop
working and start taking care of the house. Realizing this was a lot to ask
of his wife and not wanting it to be a deal-breaker, he compromised to let
her finish out the school year. Happy about getting his wife out of what
he concocted in his head to be a spider web of her principal's affection, he
did not consider the financial toll it would take on the household to not
have her income to support all her habits. He knew he couldn't ask her to
stop enjoying the small pleasures that she indulged in, and so not wanting
to rock the boat, Viraj tinkered with the idea of selling his property. His
business mind quickly took that option off the table and thought about

going back to selling the green stuff. With it almost legal in most states, he didn't see the harm in selling a little weed. Luckily, he didn't have to make a decision right away, so tucked the idea away in his back pocket for later.

CHAPTER
TWENTY-TWO

Milagro

PRISCILLA WAS HOSING DOWN the sidewalk and flushing the leaves into the gutter when she noticed an apparition walking down the block carrying a navy blue and yellow duffle bag and dragging a roller bag by its handle behind her. At first, Priscilla didn't pay it any mind but as the silhouette got closer, she realized that the stringy ponytail that was hanging over the girl's shoulder stuck in the duffle bag strap, and the wide hips that the bag kept bouncing off of on the left, belonged to her daughter, Milagro.

"Milagro," Priscilla whispered and then repeated much louder, "Milagro!" Priscilla dropped the hose without thinking about the water running out and onto the sidewalk as she wiped her hands into her pants and ran toward her daughter. "Oh Milagro, que linda, how beautiful you look. It is so good to see you," she said as she threw her arms around her daughter in pure joy.

Milagro was generally happy to see her mother but was battling a depression that made it difficult for her to express her emotions.

"Where are you coming from?"

"I took the city bus then walked a few blocks to get here. I mapped it after you gave me the address and it wasn't hard."

"Mapped it. You kids know all the technology. How long did it take?"

"I got a ride from my school to Fremont Street. It was only about an hour from there."

"Fremont Street, mi amor, it is dangerous over there."

"Well, that is where the best bus to catch was. I just got dropped off, waited ten minutes and the bus came. I've never been down there before."

"Aye, okay. Stay away from those parts. It's unsafe.

Milagro heard the words dangerous and unsafe and became intrigued. What could be so bad about Fremont Street, she wondered. She didn't see anything sinister in the ten minutes that she spent standing at the bus stop. The directive to not go from her mother piqued her interest. The warning enticed her. She wouldn't venture out to those parts anytime soon, but Fremont Street was definitely on her mind.

"Oh my goodness, the water is still running," Priscilla scurried toward the valve to shut off the hose. "Come, come mija. Come inside. Let me show you your room and give you a tour of la casa. Angelito is taking a nap, but you will meet him when he wakes up and the rest of the family at dinnertime. I'm so happy you are here with me."

The two entered the house through the garage and Priscila showed Milagro where they would be bunking together in the maid's quarters. "Let me give you a quick tour and then you can unpack. I cleared a draw for you and bought some extra hangers. The bathroom is there. Take a shower, get comfortable, and settle in. But first, follow me. Come on."

Priscilla was excited for her daughter to be there. She ran through the house showing Milagro the master bedroom, Angel's room where he was sleeping, and Marcella's room, which had a pile of clothes on the bed that Priscilla did not plan on folding or putting away. She showed her the kitchen and living room, as well as the hall bathroom.

"Aye. Come with me," Priscilla headed toward Nella's office.

"What's the matter?" Milagro picked up on her mother's hesitance.

"We are going to meet the woman of the house, mi patrona. Be quiet, be friendly, and mostly stay out of her way."

"Is that how you live?"

"Si pero no. But that is how you are going to have to," Priscilla gave her daughter a look of apology and then dramatically opened the sliding door that separated the house from the practice.

"Nella," Priscilla said in almost a whisper. "Nella," she got a little louder.

"Yes, in here." Nella was sitting at her desk. She did not have a client at the moment but was looking through her notes and seemed slightly perturbed.

Priscilla gave a little knock on the door and entered. "Nella, this is my daughter, Milagro," she said, a proud mother grinning from ear to ear.

"Nice to meet you, Milagro," Nella said warmly.

"You too Ms. Nella. You can call me Millie."

"Nice to meet you, Millie. I understand you will be staying with us for the summer."

"Yes, while school is out."

"You're in college, right?"

"Yes, ma'am."

"That is good. What is your major?"

"Communications."

"Oh. What do you plan to do in that field?"

"I'm not sure, maybe become a television broadcaster or a news journalist."

"That sounds excellent. Congratulations and good luck. Please make yourself comfortable yet invisible if you know what I mean."

"Yes, I told her," Priscilla jumped in.

"Yes, I know what you mean," Milagro said as she laughed at Nella's bluntness.

"Is something funny, dear?" Nella asked.

A look of panic spread across Priscilla's face.

"Nothing in particular. I'm just happy to be here and see my mom and finally meet you all who I've heard so much about."

"You've heard about us? I'd be interested to know exactly what you've heard," Nella gave Priscilla a disapproving glance.

"Well, just your names and that I work for you," Priscilla said hoping to end the conversation that her daughter was saying way too much in.

"Right," Nella caught sight of the file in front of her and remembered that she was busy trying to figure something out. "Is Angel awake from his nap, yet?"

"Not yet. Another five minutes and I will wake him," Priscilla said, knowing that Nella did not like her son to nap for more than an hour once he came home from school.

"Okay, make sure he doesn't oversleep. You can bring him here to say hello to mommy when he wakes. I am mostly free this evening."

"Okay, will do," Priscilla responded.

"Well, I will see you around, dear," Nella directed her attention to Milagro once more before turning back to her papers.

The two women walked out of the office and Priscilla closed the door gently. Milagro followed her back through the sliding doors, down the hallway, across the living room, through the laundry room, and into the bedroom that she planned to hibernate in for the next two months.

"Okay, here you go. Dresser, closet, shower, bed. All yours."

"Thanks, mom."

"You're welcome and next time I tell you to stay quiet, try not to talk so much."

"She seemed nice enough, at first."

"Yeah, that might be the trick. Just stay lowkey and beginning next week, you can start looking for a summer job."

"A job?"

"Yes, what did you think, you were going to loaf around here all day?"

"I work on campus all year long. I was hoping to relax, you know, have a summer vacation."

"Nope, not here. You need to be out of the house all day. And the extra money won't hurt. I have to go wake up Angel. I'll check on you in a few hours. Until then, make yourself comfortable."

Priscilla turned and left the bedroom to make her way across to the other side of the house. Milagro used one foot to pull the heel part of her sneaker off and then did the same on the other side. She kicked them close to the wall so they could be out of the way, and then dropped onto her mother's bed. She did want to take a shower and change her clothes, and even unpack the bags she had brought into the space that her mother was kind enough to clear for her. Unfortunately, depression began to creep up from her recently freed feet and take over her body and her mind.

Mentally and physically paralyzed from the idea of living somewhere she wasn't welcome and working somewhere she didn't want to be were too much for her to handle at the moment. She blinked slowly a few times, each time wondering when she might be able to score some weed. It was the only thing she knew that worked to take the edge off, transport her from the reality of life to something far more enjoyable. She would work that out when she woke up. For now, it was all about falling asleep and entering dreamland, the only other thing that seemed to feel good.

CHAPTER TWENTY-THREE

Shandell

"HOT TEA AND MERCY, please get me hot tea and Mercy."

"Here mom, here is some soup," Kayla entered her mother's room to see her hugging herself, rocking back and forth. Her cheeks were stained with the crust of old tears and her hair was a mess.

"Oh Kayla, thank you. I love you. I am in so much pain. Do you know if grandma got in touch with that doctor from Vegas?"

"I don't know," Kayla answered honestly.

"I need to speak to that doctor, hot tea and Mercy, please just give me hot tea and Mercy," Shandell wailed pitifully.

Kayla felt sorry for her mother at that moment. She had never understood the extent of the pain and sorrow her mom was feeling until now, as she watched her; helpless, hopeless, begging for relief.

"Kayla, I have to pee."

"Okay, what do you want me to do?"

"Hold this soup for me please." Shandell handed her daughter the bowl of soup and then attempted to slide out of the bed. "Oww, oww, oh, ooooh." The slide method hurt too much and so Shandell stopped and tried rolling, which landed her on the floor. Kayla jumped back, spilling some of the soup onto her own hands.

"Are you okay?" Kayla was mortified at the whole situation.

"No, and I'll be even worse if I don't get to that bathroom. Please help me up."

Kayla put the bowl of food down on the little nightstand after clearing a space at the edge and began the task of helping her mother up off of the floor. At one hundred and twenty pounds, Kayla could have almost picked her up like a baby and carried her to the bathroom, but instead, the two pushed and pulled and hoisted until finally, Shandell was on her feet. Using the edge of the bed and the bedroom doorknob, she wobbled her way out of the room and into the bathroom, making it to the toilet just in time. Shandell closed the bathroom door so that Kayla couldn't hear her cry as she sat there with her face in her hands, sobbing and wondering, why her?

CHAPTER TWENTY-FOUR

≈≈≈

"HEY, WHAT ARE YOU DOING?" Simone interrupted Viraj as he was quietly meditating in front of the shrine he had built for just this purpose.

Viraj opened one eye to see Simone standing there in a black dress that could have been a sundress aside from the lacey back which made it look more like a nightie.

"I'm meditating."

"Oh?"

"You ever tried it before?"

"Not really."

"You want to?"

"I don't know how."

"I'll show you. Grab one of those pillows and come and sit down.

Simone turned her attention to the corner of the room where Viraj pointed. There was a stack of different colored throw pillows of different sizes. She chose a square, sky blue pillow and brought it over to where Viraj was sitting in front of a small wooden table with two, lit white candles, a picture of Yogananda, and a framed swirly optical illusion design that seemed almost hypnotic.

"Okay," Viraj continued. "Sit up straight. Breathe in for a count of six, hold it for three seconds, and then out for a count of eight. You can start with your eyes closed and keep count, but once you find the rhythm, you won't have to count anymore. When you feel comfortable with the breath, you can open your eyes and stare at the middle of that picture," he pointed to the swirls. "It'll keep you focused."

Simone did as she was told. Viraj continued his meditation as if she wasn't there and didn't even seem disturbed by her growling stomach, which sounded louder than it was in the middle of the meditative silence. Though Simone was embarrassed by her belly music, she remained there, breathing and counting and staring.

After about ten minutes, Simone became bored and wanted to get up and leave. She wondered how much longer the session would be but didn't want to be rude and interrupt Viraj for a second time, especially after he was nice enough to invite her into his world.

Simone began fidgeting and her breath, which was once quiet and even, became shallow and loud. Viraj turned his head slightly to see Simone hunched over, staring into space and not meditating at all. Although there were still twenty minutes left until his midday hour meditation was over, he acquiesced and finished early for Simone's sake.

"How did you like it?"

"It was good. I didn't feel anything though."

Viraj laughed, "You're not supposed to feel anything. Maybe calmness or a stillness."

"Okay, I felt that but my stomach was interrupting me. Growling all loud and shit."

Viraj winced at the utterance of the curse word in his sacred space. "Get dressed and we'll go get some lunch."

The two got up and Simone went to her room to get dressed. She remembered the nugget of weed that was wrapped in tissue as the smell of marijuana hit her nose as she opened the top drawer. She wanted to smoke. She got dressed and met Viraj downstairs in the kitchen.

"I have a little nugget if you want to roll something before we go."

"It's cool. I have some stuff I can roll." With that, Viraj broke out his bag of weed and retrieved a blunt wrap from one of the kitchen drawers. He rolled a tight blunt and the two shared it before heading out.

"What do you feel like eating?" Viraj asked as he backed out of the driveway.

"I don't know. What's good around here?"

"There's a place Joan always gets food from. It's a sports bar, they have everything."

"Okay, sounds good."

The two rode to the sports bar in silence save for Kendrick Lamar's voice on the satellite station. The weed had kicked in so they just mellowed out and enjoyed the music and the ride. Just as Viraj pulled into a parking spot, his phone rang. It was Joan. He put the car in park and turned it off before he picked it up.

"Hey baby," he answered.

"Hey love, how are you?"

"Good."

"How was meditation?"

"It was good. I was a little distracted today, but still good." Simone sat quietly in the car and felt a little bad that she was the cause of his distraction. "What's up?"

"I forgot I have therapy after work today so I'm going to be home later than usual. I can pick up dinner on the way in."

Viraj couldn't help but think that his wife was going to be staying late at work with her boss. All sorts of thoughts swirled around his head as he pictured her leaning over the desk in her classroom with her skirt hiked up over her behind. He thought of her on her knees in the principal's office, pleasing him. The principal's hand on her head, pulling her hair and moaning.

Without breaking a sweat, he said, "It's cool. I'll just pick up something from that sports bar that you always get food from. I'll have dinner waiting for you when you get home."

"That is so thoughtful of you, thank you."

"What is it that you want? I'm going to head there now for lunch and just pick up dinner one time."

"Good idea. I'll have the grilled shrimp salad with ranch dressing on the side."

"That's what you usually get, right?"

"Yeah."

"I think I'll have that too. I'll get one for Simone as well."

It didn't go over Simone's head that Viraj was lying to her sister in real-time. Why didn't he just tell her that he was about to go into the sports bar and that she was with him? She didn't say anything but wondered how often Viraj lied to Joan about midday runs. She wondered if she should tell Joan the truth. As the weed moved further down into her soul, Simone began to think of Viraj as daring and sexy. This would be their little secret, a little lunch secret.

"Let's go." Viraj's conversation with Joan ended with an 'okay see you later, love you too' without Simone realizing it. The two got out of the car and went into the restaurant for lunch. Viraj did not hold the door open for Simone, which she normally would think was rude but didn't seem to care since she was high.

"This is some good weed," she said as she sat down next to Viraj at the bar.

"You want a drink?" he asked.

Without knowing it, Simone had stroked the biggest ego Viraj had, the quality of his weed. He was very proud of the grades he was able to negotiate for a good price. Since Joan didn't smoke and was actually anti-drug, the only comments she made about weed were negative. To hear Simone compliment his weed made him proud, made him happy, made him horny.

"A mimosa, maybe."

"You know what you want to eat?"

"I'll just have whatever you're having," Simone yielded to Viraj's judgment; him mistaking her feeble-mindedness for submissiveness, a quality he loved in women and wished Joan had.

"Bartender let me have two grilled chicken salads with ranch dressing and a mimosa," he ordered.

"Will that be all?"

"Also, a water with lemon for now and I want to place an order for three grilled shrimp salads to go."

"Okay, no problem," the young, Ethiopian bartender with large gold hoop earrings and long, pointed fingernails painted a hot pink wrote down the order. "Will that be all?"

"Yes."

"And an order of wings with a side of fries," Simone piped up speaking directly to the woman.

The bartender looked at Viraj who shook his head in approval. She smiled and walked to the back through the swinging door that led to the kitchen where she informed the cooks of the order and returned with a glass of water and lemons on the side. She mixed champagne and orange juice to satisfy the mimosa request and busied herself while waiting for the salads and wings to be complete.

"Here you go," she said as she set the food down in front of the couple, placing napkins and silverware on the bar, as well. "Can I get you anything else?"

"I'm good," Viraj stated.

"Hot sauce, please," Simone said, "and buffalo sauce if you have."

The two ate in silence, glancing now and then at the baseball game on the television that was mounted up on the wall. When the two were almost finished, Viraj informed the bartender that he was ready for the to-go order, as well as the check, which included another glass of mimosa.

"Here you go, sir," the bartender placed the check in front of Viraj, "and your salads along with napkins and forks are in the bag."

"Thank you," he said.

"These salads are really popular. Are they good?" the bartender engaged in a genuine conversation with her customer.

"You never had one?" Viraj asked, surprised.

"I can't, I'm allergic to shellfish. That shrimp would kill me," she responded.

"Oh, yeah, well you don't eat them then," they laughed. "But they are good. My wife comes in and gets them all of the time."

"Oh my goodness, wait, I think I know her. She looks just like you," the bartender said, pointing to Simone.

"Well, not exactly like me. That's my sister, though," Simone looked up from wiping the barbecue buffalo chicken wing sauce from her fingers and smiled.

"Yeah, I see it," the bartender said, shaking her head up and down as she looked into Simone's face. "She calls in the order and comes in to pick up the two shrimp salads to go all of the time. She's very friendly and always leaves me a nice tip."

"I'm sure she does," Viraj got up and took his wallet out of his back pocket to pay the bill, leaving a generous tip and grabbing the plastic bag containing the night's dinner.

Simone downed the last gulp of her mimosa and feeling a bit tipsy, got up from the barstool and followed Viraj out of the sports bar. "Thanks, bye," she said to no one in particular.

"Bye-bye, thank you," the bartender responded without looking up from the place she was clearing at the bar where they had just left.

As they rode back, Simone began feeling tired. Between the weed and the food, all she wanted to do was lay down for a siesta. Viraj, on the other hand, was riled up thinking about what the bartender had said. She calls in the order then comes in and picks it up. 'What was she doing with the other twenty minutes that it takes for them to make the salads?' he wondered. 'Was she meeting someone in the parking lot?' 'Was she going to someone's house?' The thoughts of his wife doing unimaginable things with faceless men ran through his head like a wildfire. Or maybe he did have a face. Maybe it was the face of the principal of her school.

Viraj pulled into the garage and tapped Simone who had dozed off in the short ride from the restaurant to the house. They both got out of the car and walked into the house.

"Thanks for lunch," Simone said as she walked across the living room and turned the corner to ascend the stairs. With her eyes barely open, she made her way to her bedroom, slipped off her shoes, and slinked underneath the covers.

Viraj barely heard her as he sat at the kitchen counter recounting the words of the bartender and conjuring up stories about his wife's adulterous acts. With his face red hot and flustered, he was about to explode. Not knowing what to do, he ran upstairs as his thoughts took over and he couldn't take it anymore. When he got to the top of the stairs, instead of turning right toward his meditation shrine, he turned left and headed down the hallway to where Simone was sleeping. He knocked.

"Simone."

"Hmmm," she muttered sleepily from underneath the covers.

"Are you awake?"

"Yeah, what's up?"

Viraj entered Simone's room and closed the door.

~~~~~
~~~~~

CHAPTER TWENTY-FIVE

~~~

KAYLA EXPERIENCED BOTH DREAD and excitement as she sat in traffic. With her two boys in the backseat kicking each other and yelling, her head was about to explode. Luckily, the baby was asleep in his car seat and she didn't have to deal with any crying. She counted her lucky stars that his needs were taken care of at the moment and decided not to say anything to the boys in hopes that they would tire themselves out before she reached the airport to pick up her grandmother.

Kayla was filled with a lot of different emotions. She was annoyed sitting in five o'clock rush hour traffic, but road rage wasn't the cause of the butterflies in her stomach. She had always known her grandmother to have it together. She drove a foreign-made car, lived in a big beautiful house, had long pretty hair, and had money. She was always composed and nothing phased her. Compared to her own mother Shandell, Kayla's grandmother was just much better at life.

Assessing herself as a single mom with three kids at the age of twenty-nine and living in an Atlanta housing project, Kayla felt inadequate before her grandmother. Although Mrs. Wright loved Kayla and her great-grandchildren, she couldn't help but express her disapproval at every turn. It was her way. It was how she dealt with Shandell her entire life and how she continued to deal with her progeny.

Kayla pulled up to the side of the curb exactly where her grandmother said she was standing. Mrs. Wright saw her and waved. Kayla opened the trunk and then got out of the car to greet her grandma with a hug. Mrs. Wright got into the front passenger side of the car while Kayla placed her large suitcase in the trunk. The boys had fallen asleep, thankfully, and now Kayla just hoped that her grandmother's loud talking wouldn't wake them.

On an uneventful ride home, Mrs. Wright talked about her flight and the lack of good customer service, even in first class. Kayla told her what was happening at home with her mom, including lots of crying, very little eating, and a lot of snappy mood swings from the both of them.

Kayla pulled up to Shandell's apartment to let her grandmother out. She gave Mrs. Wright the key and told her she would be back after she got the boys fed and bathed and ready for bed.

"Get my bag out of the trunk for me, honey." Mrs. Wright was prepared to cook for Shandell and settle in to spend the night at her house.

Kayla pulled out the luggage and rolled it to Shandell's front door. She left her grandmother there fiddling with the lock, not willing to get pulled into the chaos and drama that lay just beyond the door. She got back into her car and drove ten seconds across the parking lot to her place where she woke up her sons to get out of the car and head to the apartment. She grabbed their bookbags and the baby out of the car seat.

Exhausted from the car ride and the stress of being in the car with her grandma for an hour, Kayla plopped down on the couch and closed her eyes. Fifteen minutes later, she was awoken by her cell phone.

"Hello."

"I'm going to stay at your place tonight," her grandmother was blunt.

"Okay," Kayla said in full understanding. She hung up the phone and forced herself off the couch. Slowly she walked to the bathroom to run a bath for her sons who were watching television in their room. She then went into the kitchen to make a pot of spaghetti and fix plates for everyone. She picked up her phone and dialed the last person in her call history. "Grandma, is there food over there, or do you want me to bring spaghetti?"

"I made your mom one of those canned soups in there. I'll have spaghetti. You can come and get me now."

"Grandma, I can't leave the boys here alone. Just walk straight across the parking lot to my house. Call me when you're leaving and I'll have my head out the window."

"Okay," Mrs. Wright hung up the phone and looked around her daughter's apartment.

"How's that soup honey," she asked Shandell.

"It's good ma, thanks. I just hate that metal taste."

"Yeah, well that's what you get for buying canned soup," Shandell's mom said in a nonchalant yet accusatory tone. She didn't mean to be callous, she just didn't have the consideration or the good sense not to be. "I'm getting ready to go over to Kayla's house."

"You're not staying here with me?"

"Oh no honey, I can't stay here."

"But ma, didn't you come to be here with me? Who am I going to talk to? Ma, please?"

"I'll sit with you for a little while but then I have to go. I'll come back in the morning to make you breakfast and everything." Mrs. Wright sat down at the edge of the bed. "Move over a little."

Painfully, Shandell scooted over and propped herself up on her side so that she could eat her soup better. Her mom caressed her head. For the first time in a long time, Shandell felt safe. She felt loved and cared for. She relished the fact that her mother was there with her. The touch of another human was delightful and although the soup tasted bad, Shandell felt better and better as its warm contents soothed her throat and made their way to her belly. Shandell closed her eyes to savor the moment, which was quickly disturbed by the slight grumble of her stomach; a reminder that at some point this food would want to exit her body. Defecation was the bane of her existence and it was in those moments that she would rather be dead than breathing God's good air. Shandell started to cry.

"What the hell are you crying for?" Mrs. Wright stopped rubbing Shandell's head.

"Oh ma, sometimes I just cry."

"Well don't do that while I'm here. It scares me. I thought something was wrong with you. Like I hurt you or something."

"I'm just really happy that you are here with me."

"I am happy to be here, too." With that, Shandell's mom hopped off the side of the bed. She grabbed the almost empty bowl of soup from the portable wooden bedside table and took it into the kitchen where she placed it in the sink. She opened each cabinet until she found a box of crackers, grabbing one of the sleeves to open and place on the table next to Shandell's bed.

"Okay honey," she said as she walked back into Shandell's room. "I love you." She kissed Shandell on the forehead and put the crackers where she could reach them. "I'll see you in the morning. Get a good night's rest."

"Okay ma, thank you. Have a good night."

Mrs. Wright dialed Kayla's cell phone number as she walked out of Shandell's room. "Kayla, look out for me. I'm on my way across." She hoisted her purse over her shoulder and opened the front door so that she could wheel her suitcase out behind her. She locked the bottom lock from the inside and closed the door tight. Once she was outside, she breathed a deep sigh of relief and began walking across the parking lot from one building to the other. She looked up and saw Kayla watching her from her window. She waved and continued the sixty-second walk until she was in front of her granddaughter's building. She hoped her great-grandsons were asleep so that she could take a quick shower and lay down in peace. Even if they were awake, it was better than the alternative. She shook her head at the thought of how pitiful her daughter looked and sounded, then walked into Kayla's house.

"What's for dinner? I'm starving," Mrs. Wright said, half out of hunger and half out of discomfort for the entire situation.

"Spaghetti. Your plate is in the microwave."

"Thanks, honey. You are such a good granddaughter."

"Thanks," Kayla said with an awkward chuckle.

"Put a towel and washcloth in the bathroom for grandma so I can take a shower. Where are the boys?"

"They're asleep."

"Good."

Mrs. Wright sat down to eat her food. It was delicious. She kicked off her sneakers and for the first time since she had left Las Vegas began to relax. Just as she was heaping another forkful into her mouth, her cell phone began to ring.

"Who could that be at this time of the night? Hello," she said hesitantly as she answered.

"Ma, I peed myself."

"What?"

"I had to pee and I couldn't get to the bathroom quick enough. I peed myself."

"What do you want me to do about it?"

"Well, I'm wet."

"I am in the middle of eating and just took off my shoes. I'm about to take a shower and go to bed, honey. It ain't going to kill you. I'll be there in the morning to help you change clothes and your sheets and take a bath and everything. Just hold tight 'til morning." Mrs. Wright hung up. She turned back to her plate of food, but when she attempted her next bite, realized that her appetite was gone and she did not want to eat anymore. She placed her plate in the fridge and went into the bathroom to wash the day off of her and get ready to sleep.

In the meanwhile, Shandell could not stand the idea of sleeping in clothes wet from urine. She was sick but she wasn't nasty and she planned to maintain her pride through this ordeal. Shandell made her way around her room, getting a towel to lay on the bed and a fresh pair of underwear to change into. She maneuvered pretty well as she steadied herself on the various pieces of furniture. Standing at the side of her bed, she used one hand to slowly get the soiled panties off of her behind and down her legs. Once on the floor, she did a small sidestep out of them and steadied herself once again. Now came the hard part.

She could not sit directly on her bottom to put the clean drawers on because the protruding tumor hurt too bad. She definitely could not bend down low enough to get her feet into them. The only way to work this situation out was to steady herself on one leg as she raised the other into the panty opening and then do it again on the other side. Shandell was weak. Her legs were shaky. She was halfway through getting her right leg through when she came crashing down to the floor, bumping her head on the side of the bed and not being able to get up. Calling out to anyone was futile because there was no one there to hear her. No one there who cared.

Shandell touched her forehead where she could feel a knot forming but thanked her lucky stars that there was no blood. With not much choice, Shandy settled in on the floor, accepting the fact that that was where she would spend the night until her mom came back in the morning and helped her up. Of course, with the pain in both her head and her ass, the only thing left for Shandy to do was cry. She rocked herself back and forth, muttering the words, "hot tea and Mercy," until she cried herself completely to sleep.

CHAPTER
TWENTY-SIX

~~~~~

FOR NO PARTICULAR REASON in the middle of the day in the middle of the week, Nella decided that she wanted to have a dinner party. Perhaps she needed a release from all of the problems of her patients. Perhaps she wanted to dress up to look and feel pretty. Perhaps she needed a good reason to invite Eugene over. Whatever the reason, and she wasn't sure what it was, she texted Paulo and Marcella that she planned on cooking something nice and that they should make sure to be home and dressed for dinner by seven-thirty, sharp. She reminded her sister to invite Eugene and then canceled her own two o'clock appointment so that she could go grocery shopping for the goods she needed.

As Nella traipsed down the supermarket aisles, she realized how oblivious she was to everything that was around her at that moment. She hadn't done her own grocery shopping in years. She didn't know where anything was, and she couldn't believe the price of milk. She was appalled by the difference in price between organic food and its alternative, inorganic food.

Luckily, the grocery store wasn't too crowded and she was able to maneuver her shopping cart smoothly down the aisles with no one to pass or move out of the way for. She had decided to make chile rellenos for dinner, a Costa Rican delicacy of oven-roasted green bell peppers stuffed with seasoned ground beef, rice, and cheese, and topped with a fried egg. It was a meal that her mother used to make for her and Marcella as children. She paused as she allowed her thoughts to run on what she remembered about her mother. She was beautiful, always smiling, always happy. Nella's mother was full of hugs and kisses for them. There was no one more loving and caring and sweet than her mother that Nella knew.

There was a slight tug at Nella's heart at that moment and her eyes began to water. She quickly collected herself but not before Priscilla and Milagro came to her mind along with a gnawing feeling that she didn't recognize. Still standing in the middle of aisle four, Nella pulled out her cell phone and texted Priscilla that she and her daughter were invited to dinner tonight at the house and that they should dress formally. She ended the message by asking Priscilla to set the table for six. Just then, she decided to purchase some large, fancy, party napkins.

As she made her way to the picnic supplies aisle, Nella thought about what she should wear. Wondering what Eugene's favorite color was, she decided on a tight navy blue dress that stopped mid-thigh. It was fashioned with a silky slip underneath a see-through lace overlay. She would wear her black, strapless push-up bra and thongs for panties. She could see the sexy, red, lace G-string in her mind, but thought better of it since it completely did not match her outfit. Without realizing it, she was fantasizing about what Eugene would like.

Nella grabbed some large, gold paper napkins that almost looked like cloth ones and headed to the checkout line. As she walked down the aisle, she realized she was wet. Nella paid the cashier and left the grocery store. She stopped at the liquor store before heading home and bought the best bottles of whiskey, rum, vodka, tequila, and red and white wines that they had. Nella enjoyed alcohol and she planned to have a good time tonight.

She was giddy with excitement about cooking and having everyone over for her mother's chile rellenos.

At seven-thirty on the dot, Nella, who opted for a loose-fitting black, halter dress that angled into an upside-down triangle as it cascaded down her body and stopped at her knees in between her legs, finished buckling the strap on her black, high-heeled sandals and looked at herself in the mirror. With a red, strapless, lace bra and matching thong underneath, she felt even sexier than she looked, and she looked smoking hot. She had already put on her one-carat diamond stud earrings, her seven-carat diamond tennis necklace, and her three-carat diamond tennis bracelet. She sparkled from the neck down and truly looked like sophisticated money. She adorned her lips with a classic red lipstick, blotted and mashed them together twice, and off she went, out of her bedroom, and down the hallway. As she rounded the corner to enter the kitchen, the guests who were patiently seated in the living room waiting for their hostess to arrive, gasped.

"You wook bootiful, mommy," Angel said; the first words Milagro had heard him say in the month that she had been living there.

"Gracias, mi amor," Nella beamed as she looked around and smiled at everyone. "Thank you all for coming," she said proudly, "Let's eat."

With that, the food that she had meticulously prepared earlier in the day and placed in the warmer a half-hour before her guests were set to arrive was retrieved and served. Priscilla and Milagro had done an excellent job of setting the table and placing three vases of fresh white calla lilies around the house for an inviting and tasteful look. The gold napkins were a bit off under the gold silverware that the ladies placed out and immediately Nella wished she had gotten black napkins, which would have matched her dress and the décor better. With no one seeming to notice or care about the napkins, everyone dug into their relleno and on the first bite, made sounds of sheer satisfaction.

"Que rico," Marcella said.

"Delicioso," Eugene cosigned.

"Nella, this is very good," Paulo said.

"Thank you," Nella was still beaming with delight. "What about you Milagro, do you like it?"

Milagro was lost in her thoughts at that moment and was jolted back to reality by Nella's question. "Oh, yes, sorry, thank you. I do like it. I like it very much. It is really good. I was just tripping on Angel talking. I didn't think he could speak. I thought he had a speech problem or something."

The sound of forks and knives hitting plates reverberated around the kitchen. Nella's face turned beet red, and in that instant, the evening was ruined.

CHAPTER TWENTY-SEVEN

The Dinner

EVERYONE ATE IN SILENCE, except for Paulo who tried to lighten the mood by asking Marcella how the pregnancy was going, Eugene how work was, and Milagro how she liked college. His questions were met with short answers and long stares. Finally, he decided that it wasn't worth it to become the center of everyone's hate, so he excused himself, cleared his place setting, and took Angel to the bedroom for his bath and bedtime.

"Don't worry about it, please leave it. I will clean up," said Priscilla as everyone else began to finish their dinner and get up from the table. She did not want to clean up the kitchen; however, she couldn't stand another moment of the bitter silence and intense stares that she was receiving from Nella and her sister.

With that, Eugene, Marcella, and Nella got up and began to walk out of the kitchen. As Priscilla and Milagro started to pick up the plates, Nella did an about-face and walked straight up to Millie. Eugene and

Marcella stopped and stood in place. With her finger in her face, Nella reprimanded Milagro.

"There is nothing wrong with my son. Angel is a perfect little boy. He is learning two languages at once and so has trouble expressing himself. There is nothing wrong with him. He is not dumb, he can speak."

"Okay," Milagro said, "I was just saying that…"

"Callate, Milagro, silencio," Priscilla snapped. "Yes, Nella, of course. She spoke out of turn. She doesn't know what she is talking about. I am so sorry."

With that, Nella gave a huff and turned on her heels. Fuming, she sped past her sister and Eugene standing in the hallway, went to her bedroom, and slammed the door, slightly stirring Angel who was almost asleep by then.

"Are you okay?" Paulo asked.

"No Papi, I am not."

"Don't listen to her, she is young, she doesn't know anything."

"Oh Paulo," Nella began to cry as she sat down on the bed next to her husband, "Oh Paulo, is something wrong with him?"

"No Nella, nothing is wrong with him. Look at him, he is perfect."

"He's five years old and can only say what, ten words, maybe twenty."

"Nella, don't worry. Don't worry," Paulo put his arm around his wife. A small sensation went from his fingers to the pit of his stomach. He hadn't touched his wife in ages, and she hadn't needed or wanted his shoulder to cry on since she had caught him cheating a few years back. He felt really good as her protector right now.

"Paulo," Nella raised her head and looked into Paulo's eyes.

The sensation went from Paulo's stomach down to his thigh, "Yes."

"Can you go and get me the tequila from the kitchen, please?"

Slightly deflated, but with high hopes of being the hero of the night, Paulo, got up to retrieve the bottle of alcohol, two glasses, and lime from the kitchen.

"Are you crazy? ¿Estas loca?" Priscilla was pissed off at her daughter and could not hold in her anger.

"Mom, it isn't me. That boy has a problem and needs some speech therapy," Milagro said as she loaded the dishwasher with the plates that Priscilla had rinsed off in the sink.

"Shush, don't say that."

"What? That he needs help? Everyone here is in denial. Y'all are the crazy ones."

Before Milagro or Priscilla knew what was happening, Milagro's cheek was stinging from the slap her mother's hand had quickly planted on her daughter's face. They both stood there wide-eyed with their mouths hanging open, Milagro's hand to her cheek, Priscilla's hand covering her own mouth.

"Ladies," Paulo entered the kitchen oblivious to the tension in the air. He grabbed two glasses and put a few ice cubes in each. He cut a lime in quarters and placed them on a plate with a salt shaker and the two glasses. He grabbed the tequila and with a pep in his step that Priscilla had never seen before, he left the kitchen. "Good night ladies."

"Good night," they said in unison, still standing there staring at each other, though their hands had taken a more natural position at their sides.

"I am going to bed mija. My head hurts. We will talk in the morning. Please finish cleaning the kitchen and do a very good job. I don't need anything else to go wrong."

Priscilla left Millie in the kitchen and went to her room. Although her head was throbbing, she decided to take a hot shower before laying down for the night. Priscilla placed the last of the cups in the dishwasher, placed a detergent pod in the soap holder, closed the door, and pressed start. Milagro was so upset with her mother. She wondered how she could take their side. She wondered how her mother could have spent every day with Angel and never brought up the fact that he needed to see a specialist. She couldn't believe her mother slapped her. Blood rushed to her face and her cheek began burning all over again.

As she stood at the kitchen sink wetting the sponge she would use to wipe off the table, she thought she heard footsteps but couldn't be sure with the sound of the dishwasher going. Not wanting to face Nella again, she spent extra time at the sink with her back against the open area of the kitchen. Then she felt something, or was it someone, close behind her. She turned around and shockingly found herself standing in front of Eugene, close enough to smell the alcohol on his breath and feel the heat emanating from his skin.

Milagro felt like a deer caught in headlights. She was frozen as Eugene stood towering over her, twice her size. He took a step closer to her. Her body tensed. He pressed his body up against hers. She could feel his penis hard against her vagina. She was stuck there between his body and the sink. He leaned his head down and kissed Milagro on the neck, his hands gripping the sink on both sides of her. He brought his hands to her waist and slowly ran them up her body, groping her breasts, squeezing them, caressing them, rubbing his thumbs over her nipples, then brought his hands up her neck and onto her face, where he held her cheeks, one redder than the other and planted a wet kiss on her lips. He brought his hands back down around her neck and with his eyes piercing into hers said, "Don't worry about Nella. I'll talk to her. I like you and don't want you to leave. This is our secret."

With that, Eugene let her go, turned around, opened the refrigerator, grabbed two bottles of water, and walked out of the kitchen like Milagro wasn't even there. Milagro began shaking, then crying. She tried to walk from the kitchen to her mother's bedroom, but her knees buckled, and she fell to the kitchen floor. Crawling, she made her way out of the kitchen, across the sitting room, through the laundry room, and into her mother's bedroom where her mother lay with her eyes closed and a heating pad on her head.

"Ma," Milagro said. "Mami," she said a little louder.

"What?" Priscilla's tone was still harsh from anger.

"Ma, Eugene touched me."

"What?" Priscilla sat up abruptly causing her head to hurt even more.

"Eugene, he came into the kitchen while I was washing dishes and touched all on me and kissed me and," Milagro's mouth was dry and it was becoming hard for her to talk.

"Millie, no. No, no more trouble."

"It wasn't me, ma."

"No more. No more. Millie, you have to go. You are going to make me lose my job and then I will be homeless and you won't be able to finish school."

"Ma, it wasn't my fault," Milagro was sobbing heavily.

"I'm sorry, hija. You can't stay here. Pack your things while I finish cleaning the kitchen. You have to go mija. I'm sorry. Call a friend, call a taxi, call someone. I'm sorry."

Priscilla stumbled out of the bedroom and into the kitchen where she tried to scrub the table hard enough to rid away the events of the night. She believed her daughter. She wanted to take one of the steak knives, head into Marcella's room, and slit Eugene's throat but she couldn't. She couldn't lose her job. She couldn't kill a man. She couldn't go to jail. Oh, what a mess this had turned into. Where was she sending her daughter at nine o'clock at night? Where was she sending her for the rest of the month?

Priscilla was mopping the kitchen floor with her head down and tears in her eyes when Milagro slinked out of the front door with just her book bag filled with some socks, underwear, and one change of clothes. She had money in her pocket that she had taken from her mother's purse. With one hundred and twenty dollars, it was enough for a cheap room and food for a few days.

Feeling sorry for herself with a swollen face and puffy eyes, Milagro headed to the bus stop that she was familiar with. She figured she could grab a taxi down to Fremont Street and rent a cheap room for the night. She would have to figure out what to do in the morning. What she knew was that it would not include calling her mother since she would never be able to forgive her. At that moment, she hated her mother and there was nothing anyone could say to change her mind.

Eugene entered Marcella's room with fire in his eyes, sex on his mind, and a hard dick in his pants. He was turned on by the fear he saw in Milagro's eyes, the power which he had wielded over her just minutes ago. He opened his pants and stood over Marcella who was sitting on the bed with her back to the headboard. She loved him and wanted to please him.

She only had eyes for Eugene, not knowing that he was a ladies' man who had his eyes on every attractive ass that he encountered.

She began to suck on his manhood, rubbing it up and down with her hand and her mouth. She swiveled her tongue on it from the base to the tip and back down again. He was enjoying it immensely. She kept going, not knowing if this was the way he wanted to cum or not. She decided to readjust herself and stopped just long enough to swing her legs off the side of the bed. He held the side of her face and pushed her closer and closer, so much that she began to gag.

Just when she thought he was going to finish, he pushed her back and raised her legs. Pulling her panties off in a quick swipe, he plunged into her, not considerate at all of her comfort or pregnant stomach. Marcella winced slightly in pain, but Eugene did not notice. She was glad. She did not want to upset him and hoped that he enjoyed all of her, even as she began to grow bigger with their child.

Marcella scratched at Eugene's back as the pressure from his penis began to build inside of her. She was in pain and began to cry out, which only turned him on more. She was glad his eyes were closed as he moved in and out of her so that he couldn't see some of the faces she made as she endured the abuse. As Marcella's cries got louder, Eugene began to grunt as he neared the end. They were so loud that Nella and Paulo could hear them in their room down the short hallway. As Nella heard the bed squeaking in the other room, and Eugene's grunts coming through the walls, she got turned on. Paulo too was turned on by the sounds of sex.

The two were laying next to each other on the bed. Nella had since gotten undressed and was laying on top of the covers in her lace underwear. She had wanted to take a shower and wash off the makeup she had adorned so lovingly to her face, but just didn't have the motivation to get back up after that long cry on Paulo's shoulder and the three, or was it four, shots of tequila.

Nella was feeling buzzed and horny, so when Paulo reached over and touched her thigh, she didn't swat it away as she had done in the past. He started to slowly massage it. Feeling courageous from the alcohol that was running through his system, he moved his hand up to her bare stomach, making sure to lightly caress her sweetness, and began making circles with his finger around her belly button. He wanted to put his mouth on her but did not want to move too fast, fearing that she would stop him.

His finger continued to make soft, sensual circles on her skin upwards until he got to her breasts. First on top of her bra and then on the bare cleavage. Touching his wife's soft, beautiful body for the first time in three years was too much for him. He couldn't help himself. Ravenously he rolled over, pulled her breasts out, and began to suck on her nipples. She moaned, to his delight, in delight. Her nipples were sensitive and stood at attention. Paulo ran his tongue down Nella's stomach and across the top of her panties. The arch in her back gave him the fuel he needed to continue. He began to munch on her vagina through her panties, soaking the material with his saliva as he licked up and down.

With a quick move, he slid his tongue to the side and found the lip just inside of her thigh. With no protest from Nella, he used his hand to move the entire panty over and began to eat her out like she was the chile relleno he had on his plate for dinner. She moaned and writhed in pleasure, making Paulo hard and horny.

With her head back, eyes closed, and a small smile on her face, Nella looked like she was in ecstasy. Taking that as a sign, Paulo pulled her panties down, slipped off his boxers, and slid on top of and into his wife. Between the buzz of the alcohol and the fantasy in her mind of being with Eugene, she didn't even realize that Paulo was moving in, out, up, and around her womanhood until a minute later when he was saying her name.

"Nella, oh Nella, oh Nella I missed you so much."

After he came, he pulled out and slid down just enough to rest his head on her. Nella opened her eyes and sat up a little to look at the top of the head of the man who had just cum inside of her; disgusted that it was indeed Paulo and not the Eugene she had seen so vividly in her mind. Paulo's sweaty face on Nella's body made her queasy.

"Comprimiso," she said to Paulo, as she pushed his head off of her and simultaneously lifted herself off the bed.

Paulo rolled over to his side of the bed and was sporting a light snore before Nella turned on the hot shower to wash her face, shampoo her hair, and scrub off the filth she felt. As the water cascaded over the suds, she tried to recall Eugene's face and body in her mind. Mixed with the shower water, tears began to stream down her face as she faced the reality that Eugene belonged to her sister and she belonged to Paulo.

CHAPTER TWENTY-EIGHT

The Next Morning

THE NEXT MORNING PROVED to shape up very differently for everyone who attended Nella's party the night before. Eugene woke up early and went home to shower, dress, and go to work. Marcella found herself on the phone calling her doctor to schedule an appointment after she sat on the toilet for five minutes staring at a bloody piece of toilet paper after her morning pee. She was legitimately worried and wanted to make sure that everything was alright with the baby. Priscilla who had tossed and turned all night and who still had a splitting headache took Angel to school and attempted to get in touch with her daughter, whose phone kept going to voicemail. Priscilla found herself sitting alone in the park near Angel's school, dreading the return to Nella's house and worried sick about Milagro.

Milagro woke up in a dodgy motel that she was able to secure for thirty-five bucks for the night. She calculated a three-night stay with food before she would have to make other moves, but once she noticed that she didn't have her phone charger, she realized that her stay would have to be cut down to only one more night so she could buy a new one. The shower and night's rest did her some good but she was still a little shook up about her encounter with Eugene. She didn't hate her mother this morning, but she was still very upset and did not want to talk to her.

Paulo had an extra pep in his step this particular morning with an accompanying whistle to go with his cheery demeanor. "Where is everyone?" he mused out loud as he danced around the kitchen scrambling eggs and pouring orange juice, only slightly realizing that there was no one there to share his joy with.

Nella woke up late and hungover. Worse than that, she had an uneasy feeling in the pit of her stomach. It was not usual for her to remember dreams, but as she opened her eyes, she lay there recounting the images and events of the dream that was clear in her head from just moments before.

She had walked into the hospital room where Marcella was laying on the bed holding her newly born baby. As Nella walked toward her with outstretched arms, the bundle in Marcella's arms became snakes. As Nella jumped back away from the serpents, similar slithering creatures began to emerge from her own stomach. Still attached to herself, the snakes landed on Marcella's bed and began to coil around her ankles and engulf her legs and thighs. The bundle coiled around Marcella's arms and neck, slowly beginning to strangle her. Some of the snakes emerging from Nella's stomach reached up and began strangling her as well.

That is when Nella opened her eyes, blinked a few times, and touched her stomach. At that point, she remembered Paulo's sweaty cheek laying there the night before. She began to recall the events of the night. Milagro's words about Angel. Marcella and Eugene going at it. Paulo sucking all over her body. She sighed and rolled out of bed.

As Nella brushed her teeth, she looked in the mirror and realized that she did not look as bad as she felt. She applied concealer under her eyes to reduce some of the puffiness from the previous night's crying and then foundation, eyeliner, and lipstick. With her hair in a high ponytail, she put on a blue pants suit with a white silk shirt and a string of pearls. She adorned her face with black-rimmed glasses and her feet with navy blue pumps. Nella looked smart as she walked down the hallway of her home, bypassing the entrance to her office where her client had been waiting for thirty minutes and into the kitchen to make herself a cup of coffee.

Just as she entered the kitchen, Nella's phone rang.

"Hello," she answered.

"Hello, may I speak to Dr. Merced, please?"

"This is Doctor Marianella Merced."

"Hello, Dr. Merced. My name is Diane Wright. I am the mother of Shandell O'Brien. I am looking for the doctor who treated my daughter a year or so ago and I found your card with her other medical paperwork."

"Shandell O'Brien, I am not sure I remember that name. I will need to look her up in my files and call you back. Can I take your phone number?"

"Sure." Mrs. Wright gave Nella her phone number as well as the phone number for Shandy.

"Okay, got it. Is she alright?" Nella asked before hanging up with Shandell's mother.

"No, not really. Her cancer has come back and she keeps asking me to find the doctor who treated her when she was in Las Vegas.

"Cancer," Nella said. "I don't think you have the right person, Mrs. Wright. I am a psychiatrist, not an oncologist. I wouldn't have been the one to treat your daughter."

"Oh dear. Okay, well, I sure was hoping that I found the right person since your card was with all of her other papers."

"You can call the hospital that she was discharged from and ask them for the name of her doctor. With her birthdate and social security number, they can look her up and get you that information," Nella suggested.

"Okay. Thank you, Dr. Merced. You have been very helpful."

"You're welcome. Good luck."

"Thanks," Mrs. Wright said.

"You are welcome," Nella said as she hung up feeling slightly worse than she already did.

In dire need of a cup of black coffee with lots of sugar, Nella wondered where Priscilla was when she realized that nothing had been brewed. Not having the patience to make a fresh pot, she took a shot of tequila to deal with the lingering hangover and onset of depression and walked confidently into her office where Joan was patiently waiting for her, Kleenex in her hand.

CHAPTER TWENTY-NINE

Joan

"JOAN, I'M SORRY I'M LATE. Rough morning. How are you, dear?" Nella entered and sat down.

"Not well, doctor. I have also had a rough morning."

"Tell me about it. You have been out of work for the summer, right? Did you put in your resignation?"

"My husband is cheating on me," Joan blurted out as she burst into tears. It took everything in Nella not to break down crying right alongside her client.

Nella blinked a few times to collect herself and wished she had that cup of coffee to settle her. "Are you sure?"

"Yes, I am pretty sure," Joan paused. "And I'm pretty sure," Joan paused again, choking up, "That it is with my sister." Nella almost fell out of her seat. "And, I put in my resignation last week," Joan buried her face in her hands and began balling. Nella started crying too.

When the two of them had collected themselves, Nella invited Joan into her home where Nella brewed a fresh pot of coffee and the two sat on her living room couch talking like old friends. Nella was careful not to disclose her personal issues or problems to her client but she let Joan talk and vent as though there was no time limit. And there wasn't. Almost two hours later, Joan had hesitantly told Nella how she found an empty condom wrapper in her sister's bedroom trash can as she cleaned up the house.

Thinking that it was strange for her sister to have met someone new and not mentioned it; along with bringing him to the house, Joan decided to rewind the cameras and see who had been coming in and out of her house while she was away. After a lengthy review of a week's worth of footage, Joan realized the only cars pulling up to the house were the mail truck, her own, and that of her husband. Simone wasn't bringing anyone to the house because the man she was sleeping with already lived there. Simone was sleeping with Viraj and Viraj was sleeping with Simone. The two of them, right there in her house.

By the end of the conversation, Joan had informed Nella of her decision to leave Viraj and file for a divorce immediately. Although Nella tried not to give her opinion but rather allow her clients to come to their own conclusions about the best course for the direction of their lives, she found herself agreeing with Joan and told her that she thought it was the right choice.

"How could she covet my husband, my own sister?"

Nella winced at the innocent yet piercing question that Joan posed. "Joan, we have to wrap up for today. You are strong and you will get through this."

"I know I will. It just hurts so much to be betrayed by two people who are so close to me; who I love."

"I know it does. What doesn't kill you will only make you stronger."

"You're right, Dr. Nella. Thank you." Joan got up from the couch and thanked Nella for the session, her time, and the coffee.

"You are quite welcome, my dear. What are you going to do for the rest of the afternoon? What is your plan? Your next steps?" Nella asked genuinely curious.

"I'm going to call my principal and ask to rescind my resignation so I can have my job back."

"Good idea."

"I am going to rent a room in a nice hotel on the strip for a week while I search for an apartment."

"Okay, good plan."

"I am going to sleep late in the mornings and take long baths at night. I am going to cry hard and eat ice cream fast. I am going to sit in the dark until I find my light. Then I'm going to get massages and spa treatments, my hair done, and my nails manicured. Go apartment hunting and furniture shopping. Call a lawyer and file for divorce. I am going to allow myself to feel every bit of this pain until it hurts too much to stay there. I will be happily miserable, then miserably happy, then just plain 'ole happy. It'll take some time, but I'll get there, with your help of course."

"It doesn't sound like you need my help, Joan. You sound self-actualized."

With nothing left to say, Joan stepped toward Nella and hugged her. Without realizing it, Nella needed the hug just as much as Joan did. The two embraced for a significant amount of time and when they released each other, each of them had tears in their eyes.

"Thank you, Dr. Nella," Joan said.

"Thank you, Joan," said Nella as she walked her toward the front door.

Joan left feeling a lot better than when she had arrived. As she headed toward the strip to find a nice hotel to stay in for the week, she decided to swing by the bar and grill restaurant near her house to pick up her favorite grilled shrimp salad.

CHAPTER THIRTY

Kayla

"DID YOU GET IN TOUCH with that doctor, grandma?" Kayla asked as she changed her mother's bed sheets.

"I can't locate the doctor that your mom is talking about."

"We have to find him, it might be her only hope."

"Well, you know with her being in hospice now, there isn't much more we can do. There isn't much more time."

Kayla choked back tears. She couldn't stand hearing that her mother was dying. She wasn't sure why, but anytime her grandmother or the nurses mentioned it, there were pangs of guilt that ran through her. Kayla had been feeling sorry for herself over the past few weeks thinking about what life would be like without her mother. It hurt her to the core that her kids would grow up without a grandmother and never have a chance to know Shandell. It pained Kayla to think about how badly she had treated her mother over the years, months, weeks, now that she was in her last days. Kayla was lost in thought of how to make things up to her mother, but she couldn't think of anything.

"Get in touch with your brother and let him know that your mom is in hospice and he needs to come and see her."

"I told him."

"When?"

"I texted him when she first went."

"Did he respond?"

"No."

"Well, call him. He needs to come and see her."

"I don't think he's going to."

"Oh, that boy is so stubborn. I might have to call him myself."

"Yeah that would be a better idea," Kayla did not want to have the awkward conversation with her half-brother about Shandell never being there for him so he did not care about being there for her. She had been in touch with him throughout the whole ordeal and on days when he was feeling himself or feeling bad about himself, he might even say that she deserved it. Kayla loved her brother and understood where he was coming from but she loved her mother and did not like hearing him disrespect her. She preferred not to talk to him at all about the situation, opting to text or email him whenever possible.

"Does she have life insurance?" Mrs. Wright asked her granddaughter.

"How would I know?" Kayla responded.

Mrs. Wright shook her head in pure disappointment and finished placing Shandell's folded clothes into a box. Shandell's apartment was already pretty bare, so the two were moving her belongings into Kayla's apartment across the parking lot. They had decided that there was no need to continue paying rent for Shandy's apartment since she was now living at the hospice facility. Mrs. Wright and Kayla had plans to visit Shandell that afternoon, right after lunch and before Kayla had to pick the kids up from summer camp. It would be a short visit, as usual, since that was all either of them could take.

Between Shandell begging for hot tea and mercy, and the other patients wailing, moaning, and crying, neither Mrs. Wright nor Kayla could stand to be there longer than thirty minutes on a good day. Although

Shandell was happy to see them when they came to visit, their abrupt departure saddened her and often left her in tears. The nurses usually took those tears to mean pain and consequently they increased the dosage of Morphine that dripped into her vein from the IV. Unfortunately for Shandell, with each increase, although she enjoyed the elimination of any pain she may have been feeling, combined with the euphoric high she received from the drug, it also sped up the process of her organs shutting down. If this continued, she would be dead in a week.

CHAPTER
THIRTY-ONE

~~~

NELLA SAT WITH EUGENE AT THE ISLAND in the kitchen
having coffee and talking about nothing in particular. He was there to see
Marcella who had asked him to go with her to the doctor that afternoon.
Too busy to be bothered with sitting in a doctor's office all day, he said
he would meet her at the house after the appointment. His phone rang.

"¿Que tal?"

"Hi, love. I am leaving the doctor now."

"Oh good. What did they say?"

"They said I am okay. And the baby is okay. But to be on the safe side,
I should not have sex for the next thirty days."

"No sex for thirty days. Are they crazy?"

"It's for the baby."

"Yes, yes of course. That is no problem."

Marcella breathed a sigh of relief knowing how much Eugene liked to have sex and not wanting to do anything that would compromise their relationship, especially at this very pivotal point.

"Okay, well I'll be home in about forty minutes. Are you still coming over?"

Not letting on that he was already in fact sitting in her kitchen, Eugene played it cool and took the out that Marcella unknowingly gave him. "I think it would be best for the baby if you got your rest. I will see you soon."

Marcella's heart sank but she did not want to argue with Eugene and give him more of a reason to stay away. "Okay love. Well, I can't wait to see you. And remember, even though the chocha is off-limits doesn't mean that the boca is."

The thought of getting head made Eugene's penis pulse. "Oh, baby I like the way that sounds. I'll see you soon. I love you." Eugene hung up, stood up, and stretched.

"More coffee?" Nella asked as she grabbed both empty cups.

"No thanks, I'm going to get out of here."

"So soon? I thought you were waiting for my sister. What did she say the doctor said?"

"Well, she is on her way. They said she is fine but can't have sex for a month."

"That's not long."

"For who?"

"I haven't had sex in years," Nella stated matter-of-factly.

"Years? You're crazy. I couldn't do it."

"It's easy when you don't have anyone you want to be with," Nella was speaking of Paulo and selectively forgetting the other gentlemen callers, few though they were, that she had entertained over the years.

"That is kind of sad, especially for a beautiful woman such as yourself."

Nella and Eugene were standing directly in front of each other. He was looking down at her and she was peering up into his eyes. Either of them could have turned away. One of them should have. "Well, no need to stick around," Eugene said as he bent down to give Nella a cheek-on-cheek kiss as was customary in Latin homes.

It is unclear who took the step that brought them two inches closer, or who angled their face so that their lips touched where their cheeks should have met. It is uncertain if Eugene wrapped his arm around Nella's back before or after Nella placed her hand on his waist. No one can be sure whose tongue pushed itself into the other person's mouth. What was certain was that in no time, Eugene had lifted Nella onto the island and sat her in front of him. He stood between her open legs. They kissed long and hard. He held her head in his hands and slowly massaged the back of her neck. He ran his fingers through her hair and gently tugged it from behind her head. As they kissed, she opened his shirt and ran her hands over his chest. He did the same to her. She breathed deeply. Her breasts, still covered by her purple silk bra, raised on the inhale and fell on the exhale. Eugene looked at her beautiful cleavage and contemplated his next move. His hands slowly began to make their way up her back, his sights set on unfastening the clasp on her bra strap.

Just then the sound of the garage door opening was heard by both of them. He stopped. She jumped off the counter and scurried down the hall to her room, fastening each button of her shirt as she moved. "Let yourself out," she yelled behind her.

"Okay. Hasta luego," Eugene said as he finished buttoning his shirt, making his way to the front door. Eugene was unsure of who he would be coming up against on the other side. If it was Milagro or Priscilla it would be a quick hello with no explanation. A quick flash of himself at the sink with Millie came to his mind and he winced. He didn't think it would be Marcella coming in from the doctor that soon but if it was he could say that he came by to surprise her; that would be easy. The only other person who was left was Paulo.

Eugene opened the door and saw Paulo sitting still in his car with his eyes closed. Eugene walked over to the driver's side door and knocked on the window, startling Paulo out of his half slumber.

"¿Que tal hermano?" Eugene greeted him.

With the car engine already off, it was easier for Paulo to open the door and shake Eugene's hand rather than open the window. As Paulo pulled on the door handle, Eugene's body blocked the door and Paulo was trapped inside the car. Eugene used his weight to push the door back, closing it onto Paulo's knee that was angled to exit the vehicle. Paulo winced at the slight tinge of pain but said nothing, to maintain an air of machismo.

Once past the car door, Eugene waited for Paulo to open it and get out, which he did. The two shook hands and engaged in momentary small talk, where Eugene informed Paulo of Marcella's doctor's visit and his desire to leave before she got there. Paulo laughed with him though he did not agree in the least bit with Eugene's logic. The two bid each other goodbye and Paulo closed the car door and went into the house.

The house was eerily silent. He walked across the living room and into the kitchen where he hung his keys on the hook made specifically for that purpose. Paulo eyed the two cups of coffee in the sink and decided to rinse them out quickly. As he stood over the sink, the pain in his knee registered. He turned off the water and bent over to rub it. Just then he was overcome with a panic attack.

Sweating profusely, Paulo's mind involuntarily flashed back to the Saturday afternoon thirty years prior when he was cleaning the pool at his principal's house in Nicaragua. Standing there in his Las Vegas kitchen, he could palpably feel the hand on his shoulder. It was heavy but gentle. He was guided to the stucco ground, not fiercely, but with enough strength to force him to his knees. His principal, Mr. Vasquez, was behind him. He thanked him for doing such a good job, for being such a good student and a good boy. He pulled young Paulo's swim trunks down from behind and told him to relax, to enjoy the peace and tranquility of the blue sky, the green trees, the birds chirping, and the man who takes care of his family, who could make his dreams come true. Paulo closed his eyes and clenched his jaw tight as Mr. Vasquez penetrated his anus. In and out he went, taking Paulo's innocence and manhood from him. Paulo had tears in his eyes, which he quickly wiped so Mr. Vasquez wouldn't see them. When he was finished, he pulled out and hugged Paulo from behind, lingering a little longer to express his gratitude. He pulled Paulo's trunks back up over his bottom and caressed his stomach as he brought his arm from around him.

"I have something important to take care of for the rest of the afternoon. You can go for a swim if you'd like. Let yourself out and lock up behind you. The money will be on the kitchen table," Mr. Vasquez said as he got off of the young Paulo, leaving him bewildered.

Paulo remembered turning over and laying on his back, the pain in his anus muted by the pain of his left knee which had been scraped on the ground to the point of broken skin and blood. As he stood there in his Las Vegas kitchen taking deep breaths to gain control back over his body and mind, the words of his principal echoed in his ears. *Thank you for being such a good boy.* At that moment, Paulo dropped to his knees and then curled up on the kitchen floor in a fetal position, holding his legs to his chest and rubbing the knee he had bumped on the car door, though it no longer hurt.

CHAPTER THIRTY-TWO

～～～

PRISCILLA WENT ABOUT THE DAY in a haze. She ran errands outside of the house for most of the day, not wanting to run into Nella or confront the events of the previous night. She was worried sick about Milagro and indifferent towards Angel for no other reason than her current feelings towards his mother. With it getting dark and nothing left to do, Priscilla grudgingly trudged her way back home with Angel.

"Angel, why don't you talk?"

"Talk," he repeated her last word.

"Exactly. You need to talk."

"Talk," he said again.

"Stop saying talk and talk," Priscilla yelled facetiously.

"Stop," Angel said, repeating a familiar word.

"Okay, I'll stop it," Priscilla chuckled.

"Stop it," Angel said again to which Priscilla didn't respond. "Juice. Want juice."

"I want juice," Priscilla encouraged him to speak in a full sentence.

"I want juice," Angel repeated.

Priscilla handed him the sippy cup that she held. Angel took it happily and began to drink. "Thank you," Priscilla chided.

"Thank you Preesy," he said sweetly.

"You are welcome, baby."

"You are welcome baby," he repeated.

"There is nothing wrong with you, is there? You just don't have anyone paying you any attention." Priscilla spoke to the oblivious Angel. "No, there is nothing wrong with you, sweet boy."

Angel continued drinking his juice and began to blink his eyes slowly as though he was getting sleepy. Priscilla noticed and debated whether or not to let him take a nap when they got home. Her cell phone buzzed. "Hello."

"Hi, mom."

"Milagro, mija. Are you okay?"

"I'm fine. My phone died."

"I've been calling you all night."

"I am okay. I stayed in a little motel near the bus station."

"Mija, it is dangerous over there."

"Well it was cheap and I had nowhere to go."

"I know Millie, I am sorry. I am so sorry."

"I don't have any money ma. I don't know what to do."

"Can you get back over here? We can discuss everything and see what we can do to make things better. When does school start again?"

"Mom, I don't want to go back to school. I hate it. I am going to quit and get a job."

"No mija. You must finish school. That is the whole point of everything."

"Mom, I don't want to finish."

"Millie, just come here and get some money and we can discuss school and everything else. Okay?"

"Okay. I'm going to come after dinner when everyone goes to bed. I'll call you when I'm outside."

"Okay, perfect, mija. Be safe. I'll see you later."

"Bye."

Priscilla hung up the phone feeling so much better. A weight had been lifted off of her shoulders knowing that Milagro was safe. This talk about not going back to school was another chink in the armor but she felt confident that they would get through it.

With a sigh of relief, Priscilla picked Angel up and carried him into the house. It was kind of late for a nap, but she decided she would put him down and let his parents deal with it if he was up all night. As Priscilla walked through the living room with Angel in her arms, she noticed what looked like the top of someone's head on the floor in front of the kitchen sink, projecting out from around the island. She took Angel to his room, placed him on his bed, and took off his shoes. She left him there with his bedroom door open, noticing that Marcella was not home and Nella's room door was closed with the television on behind it.

Priscilla went back to the kitchen to inspect the contents on the floor; it was Paulo. She walked around him and tapped the arm that was closest to her, still wrapped around his updrawn legs. "Paulo. Paulo, are you okay?"

He slowly came to consciousness, blinking his eyes and seeing the blurred outline of Priscilla's body leaning over him. For a minute he thought it was his mother. "Madre?"

"No, Paulo, it's me, Priscilla," she whispered. "You passed out. Are you feeling okay?"

Paulo started to remember where he was and with clearer vision looked around and saw Priscilla and the kitchen. He stretched. Priscilla stood up and grabbed a glass to fill with water for him. He rolled over and began to get up. She lent an outstretched hand, which he took as he got to his feet and regained composure. She handed him the glass of water.

"Gracias," he said as he took it and put it to his mouth.

"Por nada," she responded as she turned away leaving him to figure out his life while she went to figure out hers.

"Better get dinner started," he said pretending as if nothing had happened.

Priscilla kept walking assuring him that she would never breathe a word of this scene to anyone.

After dinner, which consisted of pork chops, rice and beans, and broccoli, everyone quietly retired to their respective bedrooms. Priscilla did not eat with them but rather had tuna fish and crackers in her bedroom. Angel remained asleep and neither Paulo nor Nella seemed to notice that the customary one-hour allotment for his nap had expired forty minutes prior. Marcella thanked Paulo for the delicious meal and went to her room to call Eugene who she missed and had really hoped to see that evening when she got home from the doctor's office. Paulo cleaned up the kitchen, took a shower, and went to sleep early, feeling surprisingly calm and lighthearted. Nella put a small bowl of rice, beans, and broccoli to the side in case Angel woke up hungry and then nursed a bottle of rum with a cola chaser. She was happy that both Angel and Paulo were asleep and she took this time to watch novelas on her tablet using her earphones so she didn't disturb anyone. The house was quiet and Priscilla kept an eye on her phone so that she wouldn't miss Milagro's call.

As Millie waited at the bus stop, she couldn't help but think about what had happened the night before. The piercing stare from Nella, the slap from her mother, and of course, Eugene. His breath, his sweat, his hands, his mouth all over her. She was disgusted with herself for not doing anything, for not saying anything, for not fighting him off. And her mom. She thought about her mom taking his side, taking the whole family's side against her. Mille's face burned hot. She was so upset she didn't know what to do. And now, she found herself standing at the bus stop to go back to that house. A wave of exhaustion fell over her. She did not want to discuss anything with her mother. She just needed some money to hold her over until she got a job of her own. She had already made up her mind that she wasn't going back to school and of course, she could not stay with her mom anymore.

Deep in thought, Millie began pacing back and forth in front of the bus stop when a long, shiny, camel brown Buick Electra rolling on spinning rims pulled up. "Hey lil mama," the smooth voice behind the wheel startled Milagro.

"Excuse me?"

"I said what's on your mind, lil mama?"

"Just waiting on this bus," she responded with a toughness to prove she wasn't scared.

"Aww man, you'll be waiting all night."

Millie's heart sank. She didn't have enough money for a room for another night so couldn't afford for there not to be any more buses running. She should have left earlier, she thought to herself.

"I can take you where you need to go," the guy said. "I'm Rollo by the way."

"No thanks, I'll be okay."

"I don't bite lil mama but suit yourself." With that, Rollo pulled off.

Millie waited another fifteen minutes before texting her mom that she was waiting on the bus and would be there soon. It was after ten and the prospect of a bus showing up was beginning to look bleak. Rollo pulled back up to the bus stop just as Millie's phone buzzed with a text message response from her mother.

"Still waiting lil mama?"

"Yeah."

"I got you some In and Out. You can eat it out there or in here if you'd like. I can take you where you're going and get you there safely."

Milagro thought about her options for a second and decided to get in with Rollo. He handed her the bag of food. "Put your seat belt on lil mama. What's your name?"

"Milagro. My friends call me Millie."

"Milagro. That's different. You Spanish or something?" Rollo asked as he pulled off.

"Yeah, my mom is from Costa Rica. It means miracle."

"Okay, I like that. Maybe you could be my little miracle. Where we headed Millie?"

"Go north, let me get the exact address." Millie opened the messages on her phone to ask her mom for the exact address of Nella's house. She remembered she had a text. It read *Take a cab. I will pay for it when you get here.* Millie wrote a reply. *It's cool, I am getting a ride. What is the address?*

Priscilla did not like the sound of Milagro getting a ride and wanted to know everything about who she was with. *Getting a ride from who? Where are you?* She quickly followed that text with the address and waited.

Millie told Rollo the address and then sent a text response to her mother. *Oh now you care? You didn't care when Eugene was touching on me.*

"Who you going to see lil mama?"

"My mother."

"You live up there with her?"

Millie took a bite of the hamburger that Rollo had bought her from the fast food restaurant chain. "No, I was just staying with her for the summer but that's over. I just need some cash so I'm going to holla at her real quick."

"If cash is what you need, I got you."

"I can't take your money."

"Why not?"

"You don't even know me like that to be giving me your money. Anyway, I need a bunch of cash."

"Like how much?"

"Like a thousand dollars."

"Dang lil mama, you got some high expenses," the two of them laughed as Millie filled her mouth with the special cut French fries she pulled from the paper bag.

"They're good, huh?" Rollo asked.

"Yeah, you want some."

"No thanks, I already ate. Tell you what," he said after a moment, "I have three hundred in my pocket. It's yours if you want it. I'll give you my number and you can call me when you have it to pay me back."

"That's nice of you, but it isn't enough. I need enough to live off of until I find a job."

"A job. That's what you're looking for? Why you ain't say that to start. I employ womens all the time."

"Oh yeah, doing what?

Rollo kept driving toward Milagro's mother's place as he explained the game. Working for him, she wouldn't want for anything. She would have a place to stay, food to eat, new clothes, new shoes, money in her pocket, hair, nails and toes done, and her cell phone bill paid. She could work her own hours and as long as she turned ten tricks a day, she was free the rest of her time.

"That doesn't sound that bad," Milagro was mostly sold on the idea.

"Womens love working for me. I'm a lover, not a fighter. I don't hit no one, I don't scare no one. I'm your provider and your protector. No one will mess with you once they know you're with me." Millie was completely sold on the idea just as Rollo pulled up to the curb in front of Nella's house. "Is this the place?"

"Yeah it is, but I don't think I need to go inside."

"You can at least go say hi to your mama."

Milagro pulled out her cell phone and sent her mother a text message. *Hi ma. Change of plans. Found a job at Rollo's. Will be in touch.*

"I'm good," she said to Rollo as she rolled down her window and dropped the crumpled bag of trash onto the ground on the sidewalk outside of Nella's house. "Let's roll."

With that, Rollo peeled off. Priscilla heard the tires and looked up from her phone where she sat teary-eyed after reading the message her daughter had sent her. It was all too familiar, and a nauseous feeling settled in the pit of her stomach. Before she knew it, Priscilla let out a yelp as she fell to her knees, grabbing her Rosary and praying in earnest for God to bring her baby back home to her safe and sound.

CHAPTER THIRTY-THREE

"AYE, DIOS MIO," Nella was spending her Saturday morning trans-
ferring paper files to her new online filing system. She was sure it would
make life easier in the future, as the salesperson at the store told her;
however, right now, it was tedious, confusing, and boring.

Having already completed her clients with last names beginning with
A, B, and C, she decided to make things more fun and go to the end of
the alphabet. There were only two clients with Z last names, a few with Y
and none with X. Nella was flying through the files and started to feel ac-
complished. By noon she was on clients with the last name beginning with
W. Walker, Wasserman, Waters, White, Womack, Wright. She paused at
this client. Shandell "Shandy O'Brien" Wright. Nella was confused at the
way the client filled out her intake form. She perused the entire document
and saw that Diane Wright was the mother and Shandell O'Brien was

her client. The names were all mixed up and the memories of Shandy came rushing back to Nella.

Shandy was a cancer patient who was referred to her so that she could talk about the things that were hurting her from deep down. Her childhood. Her mother. Her stepmother. Her beloved father. Her son who was taken from her as a baby and given to her aunt. Shandy wanted to be skinny. Shandy wanted to be loved. Shandy just wanted hot tea and needed her doctor Merced.

"Dios Mio!" Nella whispered to herself realizing that it was Shandy's mom who had called her weeks, maybe months ago. She rummaged through her desk to find the paper she had written the phone number on and realized she didn't have it. She looked at the file. Under emergency contact was Diane Wright, mother. A phone number was listed. Nella called it. It was a landline answering machine. She left a message and continued looking through the file. Kayla O'Brien, daughter. There was a number that Nella made a last-ditch attempt to call.

"Hello," Kayla answered.

"Hello, this is Dr. Marianella Merced. Is this Kayla O'Brien?"

"Yes, it is."

"Oh, thank goodness. I am the psychiatrist who treated your mother Shandy, well Shandell, a few years ago. Your grandmother called me and said Shandy wanted to speak with me. Is she available?"

"Um. You said this is Dr. Mercy?"

"Yes, Dr. Merced."

"Hold on a second."

Nella held her breath as she waited for Shandell to come on the phone. They had a special client-patient relationship. It was like none that Dr. Nella had ever had. She both loved and pitied Shandell. She wanted to hold her and hug her while simultaneously slapping her into reality and telling her to love herself, be courageous, and enjoy the life that God had given her.

"Hello."

"Shandy?"

"No, Dr. Merced, this is Diane Wright, Shandell's mother."

"Yes, hello. Sorry it took me so long to get back to you. I was going through my files and just realized who Shandell was."

"Shandell died last week."

The silence was audible.

"Her funeral is tomorrow," Mrs. Wright finished the sentence that left Nella speechless.

"Died?"

"Yes, doctor. She passed away and is finally no longer in pain."

"I am so sorry, Mrs. Wright. My utmost condolences to you and your family."

"She really wanted to talk to you, doctor. I'm sorry she didn't get a chance to."

"You said the funeral is tomorrow?"

"Yes, it will be graveside at Crestview Cemetery, tomorrow at ten in the morning with a repast to follow."

"I will do my best to be there."

"Well, don't break your neck to get here honey, she's gone now."

"Thank you, Mrs. Wright, and again my condolences."

"Thank you, doctor."

The two women hung up the phone and Nella sat at her desk. She immediately saved everything she had been working on and clicked out of the file management software that had monopolized her morning. She logged onto a travel site and within minutes had booked a roundtrip first-class ticket on a red-eye from Las Vegas McCarran international airport to Atlanta Hartsfield-Jackson for that night returning Monday morning. She paired it with a two-night stay at a nice hotel near the airport. She did not bat an eye when the price totaled one thousand, two hundred, and ninety-nine dollars, which she put on her credit card. She straightened up her office and then went to pack a carry-on. It was three in the afternoon and with a nine p.m. flight, she had just enough time to let Priscilla know that she was in charge of Angel while she was gone, tell Paulo that she was leaving for two days, check on Marcella to make sure that she was good, and get to the airport in time to catch her plane.

With Paulo nowhere to be found, Nella assumed he was visiting with friends of the family that Saturday afternoon. She called his cell phone which rang out until it finally went to voicemail. She left a long-winded message about her old patient's mother reaching out to her, her patient passing away, and the need to travel to Atlanta, Georgia immediately. She gave him the information about her flight and where she would be staying and informed him that she would be home Monday afternoon. Four minutes later, she hung up and went to find Priscilla who had made herself quite scarce since the fateful night of the dinner.

It was technically Priscilla's time off for the rest of the weekend. Nella reconciled the additional work with the decision to give Priscilla a choice of two extra days' pay or two days off during the week. Either way, it had to be done. Angel was napping in his room with the door open, as Nella demanded. Marcella's door was closed but she could hear Eugene's voice alongside her sister's behind it. Nella walked across the house to Priscilla's room and knocked.

"Pree. Pree. Priscilla," she continued to knock though there was no answer. "Aiy," Nella said out loud with the resolve that Priscilla wasn't home. "That is so strange."

For the entire time that Priscilla had worked for Nella, she had never known Priscilla to leave the house on weekends, or never noticed. Either way, she needed her now. Nella went back to her room to retrieve her phone and call Priscilla.

"Hello."

"Hi, Priscilla. Where are you?"

"I'm down on Fremont Street."

"Oh my God, what are you doing down there?"

"What can I help you with, Senora?"

"I have to go out of town tonight, in fact, in a few hours. I don't know where Paulo is at the moment, but if you could take charge of Angelito until I get back Monday afternoon, I would appreciate it. I will pay you extra."

"Yes, Senora. It's no problema. I am on my way back now," Priscilla hung up and stopped the search for her own child to go and take care of someone else's.

With that, Nella went and knocked on Marcella's door. "Come in," her sister's happy voice sang. Nella opened the door to see Eugene and

Marcella sitting up on the bed eating from a box of meat lover's pizza that Eugene had brought from Marcella's favorite restaurant. "Do you want a slice of pizza?"

"Oh, si!" Nella said as she took a few steps to enter the bedroom. Eugene put a slice on a paper towel and handed it to her. "Gracias." She took a bite and savored the moment of all the tastes on her tongue. Everyone was smiling. When she stopped chewing and swallowed the first bite, she stated her purpose for interrupting their Saturday afternoon. "Hermana, I have to go to the airport."

"¿Aeropuerto?"

"Yes. A quick business trip. One of my clients passed away and I am going to attend her funeral in Atlanta."

"Oh, pobrecita, I am sorry to hear that," Marcella was genuinely sad to hear of the passing of her sister's client.

"Yeah, it is sad. She was a nice woman. Anyway, the funeral is tomorrow and I just found out, so I have to leave here in one hour. I don't know where Paulo is, and Priscilla is on her way back from Fremont Street."

"Fremont Street, what the hell is she doing over there?" Eugene spoke up.

"I have no idea," Nella exclaimed. "I have asked her to take charge of Angel while I'm gone, but if you can also keep an eye out and help with him, that would be great."

"Claro que si, of course," her willing sister responded.

"Paulo's not here?" Eugene confirmed what Nella had stated earlier.

"No, I don't know where he is. I left him a message."

"I can take you to the airport if you need me."

"That would be great," Nella said.

"That's a good idea," Marcella agreed.

"Okay, let me finish getting my things together and I'll be ready. We will leave in an hour." Everyone looked at the clock on Marcella's dresser which displayed a time of five forty-five.

"Got it," Eugene said as he grabbed another slice of pizza.

Nella backed out of the room and closed the door. She took a quick shower and put on a cute and comfortably canary yellow designer track-suit. As she applied concealer, foundation, and a healthy amount of red lipstick, Priscilla entered the house and made her way down the hallway to the back of the house. She checked in on Angel who was sitting up in his bed quietly watching cartoons on television. She waved to him and he waved back. She knocked on Nella's door which was partly open.

"Entra."

"Oh Nella, you look nice."

"Thank you Pri. How are you? How is Millie?"

"We are fine," Priscilla said, not wanting to broach a heavy subject before her patrona left on a business trip.

"Okay good. When I get back, let's talk about everything. Perhaps Angel does need some speech therapy or early intervention of some sort. I want to make sure that we are alright."

Priscilla was surprised at Nella's demeanor. Perhaps it was because Nella relied on Priscilla to take care of her son, or maybe it was being confronted with the death of her patient and her own mortality that gave her this change of perspective. "We are alright. I am sorry for my daughter's actions and hope we can move forward from this. Let this be water under the bridge."

"Yes, me too. Good. I am glad that is taken care of. I am leaving in five minutes. I have no idea where Paulo is today."

"Angel is awake. I will feed him and bathe him and everything. Do you need a ride to the airport?"

"Eugene is here, he will take me."

"Okay good. Let me make you a sandwich for the ride."

"I don't think there is time."

"I will be quick."

Priscilla ran to the kitchen and made two turkey and cheese sandwiches with slight mayo and slight mustard on each. She placed them in a sandwich bag and pulled out two bottles of water. She put one next to the sandwiches and took the other one to her bedroom, peering down the hallway to make sure no one was coming. Moving stealthily, she grabbed her purse and pulled the small vial she had obtained from Fremont Street out of it. She quickly opened the water bottle and dropped twelve drops, three more than the gypsy woman instructed her to, into the bottle, closing it tighter than was normal for a water bottle.

She emerged from her room just as she heard voices coming down the hallway. In three hops, Priscilla was back in the kitchen holding the bag of sandwiches and the spiked bottle of water in her hand. "All ready?"

"Yes, yes. Ready to go."

"Hey Eugene, here, this is for you," Priscilla handed him a bottle of water.

"Thank you, I am so thirsty," he opened it with a little struggle and began to drink.

"Nella, here are some sandwiches for the trip. And," she reached back to the counter, "A bottle of water for you. You must drink yours before going through security."

"Si, si. They are so strict now."

Marcella was standing there to see her sister off. Priscilla went into the pantry to get a bottle of water for her, as well. "Marcella, you need to stay hydrated, tambien."

"Yes, she does," Nella agreed. "You take care of yourself and that little one until I get back."

"I will," everyone laughed as she took the bottle from Priscilla and shook it from side to side.

"Okay, we better get going," Eugene said. He kissed Marcella, "I'll see you later."

"Are you coming back after the airport?"

"I don't think so, but I will come tomorrow after work." Marcella was visibly disappointed, but time was ticking and Eugene and Nella had to leave the house.

"Have a safe trip," Priscilla said.

"Thank you and thank you very much Pri."

"It's nothing," Priscilla said. "Go, handle your business. We will be okay here."

Marcella and Nella hugged each other and both parted ways, Marcella back down to her room and Nella out the door with Eugene.

"Have you eaten Marcella?" Priscilla yelled after her.

"Yes, we had pizza."

"And Angel."

"Nada."

Marcella audibly closed her bedroom door and Priscilla decided to make Angel a peanut butter and jelly sandwich that he could take or leave. She was pleased with her work this evening. Though she had originally gone to Fremont Street in search of her daughter, she found something that would help make her feel better since Milagro was in the clutches of the world. No one, she decided, would get away with messing with her child, no one.

CHAPTER THIRTY-FOUR

Freed

PAULO FOUND HIMSELF BACK in the Freezone where pot and prostitutes came a dime a dozen. He wasn't sure what else was traded in the area because he was never in the market for cocaine, meth, guns, or anything that would get him in trouble with the law. Paulo parked his car and wished that he could be free to be himself all of the time. He felt stuffy at his job and cornered like a small animal in his home. He wondered where he had gone wrong in his life and his mind flashed back to Mr. Vasquez who had used Paulo to express his own secret desires numerous times during his high school senior year. Paulo wondered if his old principal was still alive. His mind ran on these thoughts with no emotion. He was not mad at Mr. Vasquez and didn't necessarily need him to be dead to feel better.

The more Paulo thought about those summer afternoons of his teen-age years, taking tequila shots by the pool, and Mr. Vasquez bending him over to penetrate him, the more bothered he became. He undid the top button of his shirt and wiped his sweaty palms on the front of his trousers. Without further thought, Paulo hastily opened his car door and walked across the street into the Wild West male saloon. It was dim and smokey, with not many people in the main parlor. A lone male bartender with black eyeliner under his eyes was behind the bar. A stationary mechanical bull sat to the left with a spotlight shining right on top of it from the ceiling. An older woman in a cowboy hat and cowboy boots worked the pole that spanned the floor to the ceiling at the front of the parlor. There was no stage, just a pole.

"I'll have a Jack and Coke," Paulo said. "And a one-hour spread. Young."

The bartender picked up a white telephone from its cradle and held it to his ear. "One for one coming up," he said. With a small, satisfied look. He gave Paulo a nod of approval and commenced making his drink. "Something for the fella?" the bartender asked as he placed the cup in front of him.

Paulo thought for a moment. "How about a brew?"

"Bottle or tap?"

"Bottle."

The bartender grabbed a cold bottle of beer from the cooler and placed it in front of Paulo. Paulo pulled out his wallet and placed a one-hundred-dollar bill on the bar. He picked up his two drinks and walked through the saloon until he came to the bottom of a dark staircase. He put his foot on the first step and the sensor picked up his motion. In an instant, the stairwell was illuminated and Paulo easily walked up to the second floor where a large, bald, muscular man with tattoos wearing a leather vest and an eyepatch stood.

"Room twelve," the man said to Paulo.

"Thanks."

Paulo walked past the man and down the hallway looking at the different dark-brown wooden doors. Some were closed. Others were ajar though it appeared that no one was in those rooms. The doors had various identifiers on them indicating no rhyme or reason for their organization. Paulo passed room C, room 5, room Belvedere, and room sixty-six before finding himself in front of room 12. He took a sip of the cocktail that was in his left hand and used the nimble fingers of his right to both steady the beer bottle and turn the knob.

He walked into a clean, cozy room that looked similar to the dormitory he stayed in when he was in France. There were wooden floors that could have used a polish, and the walls were painted a dim yellow. A warm red glow illuminated the room from a colored light bulb under a shaded lamp that sat on a small light-brown wooden table that sat at the head of the twin-sized bed that spanned the length of the wall to the left. In the corner to the right was a rocking chair with a low footrest and next to it a silver metal stool. Paulo looked around the room anxiously until he finally allowed his gaze to fall upon the shirtless young man in white boxers who was laying on his side on the bed, casually flipping through a Bare Hunt magazine looking at the young naked chaps in seductive costumes and compromising positions.

"Hey," Paulo said.

The young man looked up. "Hey," he responded.

"I got you this," Paulo outstretched his arm to hand the evening's candy a beer.

The young man made no motion. "Close the door," he said.

Paulo turned and closed the door behind him. He walked over to the bed and handed the fellow the beer then crossed the room to have a seat in the rocking chair. "What's your name?" he asked as he sat down.

"Samuel, but you can call me Sammy."

"Okay, Sammy. Come take off my shoes and rub my feet, please?"

Sammy took a few gulps of the beer and then sat it on the little lampstand. He scooted off the bed and down to the floor where he seductively crawled on all fours to where Paulo was sitting with his feet propped up on the footrest. Sammy stopped in front of Paulo and began to untie the laces on his well-polished, black, name-brand shoes. He pulled them off one by one and began to rub Paulo's feet over his socks. He slowly pulled off each sock and continued to dry rub them, eliciting small squeals of delight from the highly neglected and overly sensitive Paulo. The young man walked his fingers up Paulo's leg and to his chest where he began to unbutton his shirt, exposing Paulo's chest hair and his vulnerability.

~~~~~~

Eugene pulled into the airport parking lot with Nella in the front seat. They got there in record time with very little traffic on the street and Eugene speeding the whole way. Nella was both terrified and turned on by Eugene's driving.

"Thanks so much, Eugene. I have plenty of time to get through security and settle in."

"Yeah, you can spend a little of it out here with me."

"Excuse?"

"I think about the other night in the kitchen with you all of the time."

"Oh Eugene, that was bad. We shouldn't have and we have to forget about it."

"I can't forget about it. I don't want to. I'm not going to forget about it or you."

Nella nervously fiddled with the zipper on her jacket, uncomfortable with the things Eugene was saying and the attention he was giving her.

"What about Paulo and Marcella?"

"Paulo doesn't appreciate you. He doesn't even know what to do with you, honestly. And Marcella. I love her and she is having my baby, but I wish I would have met you first."

"Eugene, you are talking crazy. You are with my sister and I am married to Paulo and that is that. There is nothing to talk about. Nothing to even think about." Nella opened the passenger side door and got out. She opened the back door of the car and grabbed her rolling carry-on off of the back seat. She was met by Eugene who had quickly exited the driver's side and walked around the back of the car to stand in front of her, the small bag and a lot of chemistry, the only things between them.

"Talking crazy, Nella. Am I?"

"Yes, Eugene."

"Tell me you don't feel anything between us." Eugene cut in front of the carry-on and placed himself between Nella and the bag. "Tell me there is nothing here."

Nella dropped her head not wanting to meet Eugene's gaze. With one finger he lifted her chin, tilting her face upwards so that her eyes met his. "Tell me," he said as he bent down to kiss her lips.

Without hesitation, Nella kissed him back and before long they were breathing heavily as they groped each other and kissed deeply. Eugene licked Nella's neck and slipped his hands up her shirt to tug on her nipples. The carry-on bag fell frontwards to the ground as Eugene pivoted the two bodies so that Nella was pinned up against the car. Nella's body stiffened. She closed her eyes, put her head down, and brought her hand up to stop him.

"We must stop," she said sternly.

"What? Why?" Eugene's erect penis was pressing against his jeans and he wanted nothing more than to feel Nella's body.

"It isn't right. This isn't right. We aren't right." Nella remembered the shock and bewilderment on her client's face as Joan recounted that her sister was sleeping with her husband. Nella remembered her own disbelief. Nella was better than this. "We are better than this."

"Oh shit Nella, come on," he said. "We're both adults."

"I can't do this to Marcella. She is my sister."

Eugene took a step back, "You're right," he said though he didn't fully agree.

Nella sidestepped from between him and the car. She opened the front door to get her purse, closed it, and picked up the small roller bag by its outstretched handle. "Thank you for the ride." She began walking toward the departure gates, never once looking back at Eugene.

Feeling a little lightheaded, Eugene walked around the back of the car toward the driver's side and got in. "Damn," he said to himself as he picked up the bottle of water Priscilla had given him at the house. He finished it off, grateful to be wetting his dry throat and quenching his thirst. "Damn," he repeated. Eugene pulled out of the parking spot and made his way out of the parking structure still wishing that he had indeed met Nella first.

The young man, Sammy, began to nuzzle Paulo's chest hair. He was in-
toxicated by the manly smell of the expensive Italian cologne that Paulo
donned especially for this occasion. Sammy began to run his tongue
across his suitor's chest, from one nipple to the other, giving each areola
a slight nibble, getting harder and more intense with each arrival.

Paulo's head was tilted back as he enjoyed the soft bites but leaned
his head down as they got harder. The smell of Sammy's hair, freshly
washed with summer breeze shampoo, aroused Paulo to full erection.
On the final and last bite, which was hard enough for Paulo to let out a
yelp, he jumped up with quick aggression and turned around, bending
Sammy over so that his elbows rested on each arm of the rocking chair.

Without hesitation, Paulo unbuckled his belt and let his pants fall
to the floor. He debated stepping out of them but decided that Sammy
would not be made love to, but rather fucked. He spread Sam's butt
cheeks and made a move to enter him from behind, but the young man
stopped him.

"Wait," Sam said much to Paulo's amazement. "Let me get some lube."

Sammy got up and walked the few steps to the nightstand where he
opened the small drawer and pulled out a little jar of Vaseline. "Do you
want to do it or should I?" Sammy innocently asked, holding out the jar.

Paulo stood there almost dumbfounded. He thought about each time
that his former principal, Mr. Vasquez, had turned him around and bent
him over. Never, not once, had he had the courage to say stop. He didn't
even know it was an option. Paulo lost his erection. He pulled up his
pants and buckled his belt.

"I can do it," Sammy said in a slight panic, not having expected the
rendezvous to be over.

"It's okay, Sam," Paulo picked up his cup and finished off its contents.

"I didn't mean to," Sammy was apologetic.

"Don't worry about it. Enjoy your beer. You won't get in any trouble.
I'm just going to call it a night."

Paulo left the room with Sammy standing there. He gave a head nod
to the bouncer who sat at the top of the steps and made his way down the
staircase that lit up at his presence. Instead of going out the same door he
came through, he decided to make a left at the bottom of the steps and

take the back exit. Although this would require him to walk around the building to get back to his car, he didn't want the bartender questioning his early departure. Not only was Paulo not upset with Sammy, he was grateful and did not want Sammy to get in any trouble.

For the first time in Paulo's life, he felt free. It seemed that the guilt that he felt about his encounters with Mr. Vasquez had taken hold of him all these years. He felt the need to satisfy some deep, dark secret within himself. Wait! Stop! Small words that held so much power. Stop. He should have used it when he was younger but didn't. He didn't know how. He wouldn't blame himself; he wouldn't continue to let a mistake of his youth cause him grief now. What he would do, was stop punishing himself. He would stop pleasing himself in a way that made him feel bad. He could stop. He wanted to stop. He would stop.

Paulo made it to his car with a new pep in his step. He was empowered by the words of the young man. No; simply no. If he would have known he could utter those words to his principal or had the courage to all of those years ago, he would be a different person. He could still be a different person. He would choose to be a different person now.

Thoughts of making amends with his wife, maybe going to counseling by himself and with her would help. He wasn't a sex addict. He didn't like young boys. He was damaged; mentally, physically, and emotionally abused. He needed a new mental schema, a new story about himself to believe, to tell, to live. He no longer had to live in the shadows of darkness that Mr. Vasquez cast over him as a teenager. It would take time but he could get better. He could reclaim that which was lost.

Paulo drove home feeling happy, feeling free, feeling like a huge weight had been lifted off of his shoulders. He resolved to go to his doctor first thing in the morning. He couldn't remember the last time he had gotten tested. He would let them draw blood and do a full STD panel. He would reclaim his manhood, his wife, his marriage, his happiness. He would reclaim his life.

Nella sat in an aisle seat on the airplane. It was dark and quiet as the plane cruised at an altitude of thirty thousand feet. Nella was only slightly tired. She was waiting for the flight attendants to make their rounds so that she could request an alcoholic beverage, both for enjoyment and to give her the slight nudge she needed to fall asleep.

As she sat there thinking, her mind casually raced on the events of the evening. She still had not spoken to Paulo and thought she would need to call him the minute she landed, regardless of the time. She thought about how lucky she was to have Priscilla there as someone that she could trust to look after Angel. Nella's heart sank a little as her thoughts turned their attention to her sweet little boy who she needed to take in for an evaluation. She was scared about what they might say, what they could diagnose. A shiver went up and down her spine and she felt the need to rub her arms for warmth and consolation.

As her hands brushed against her breasts, she immediately thought of Eugene. His touch, his tongue, his lips on her mouth. Although she wondered what it would have been like to feel him inside of her, she was happy that she stopped; that she walked away. She sighed at the heaviness of the reality that he was her sister's unborn child's father and what the future would look like for them. She knew he was off limits and resolved never to entertain him again. Nella rubbed her forehead, determined to stop thinking about Eugene. She turned her thoughts to Atlanta.

She planned to take a taxi to the hotel where she would check-in, shower, dress, grab some breakfast, and head to the graveside funeral of her former patient Shandy O'Brien. Nella's shoulders sagged as she thought about the psychological whirlwind that Shandy had gone through dealing with cancer. Nella remembered Shandy being happy that the disease had helped her lose weight and couldn't see the physical or mental sickness in her size or the emotions that she had attached to it. Nella remembered Shandy saying that she would be able to find true love now that she was smaller, though she equated love with sex, which she still couldn't attain with the tumors protruding from her bottom. Nella tried to get Shandy to talk about the relationship she had with her mother but all she ever said was 'it is what it is,' as if that made all of the hurt and pain disappear. Nella wanted Shandy to express her feelings about the mystery child, a son, that she claimed on her intake form but not in conversation.

Shandy was in a lot of physical pain and mental turmoil back then. The disease added to her mental distress by forcing her to make health decisions that she wasn't prepared to make. Scared of the horror stories she had heard about chemotherapy and having a sinister distrust of doctors, Shandy wanted to take the holistic route. She attempted different protocols that she told Nella about, but they either didn't work, or she stopped them sooner than was required to achieve the desired result. Sometimes Nella wondered if Shandy was purposely sabotaging the success of the protocols. It did not help that her mother was against any and everything Shandy proposed for her healing. If it wasn't chemo, Mrs. Wright did not want to hear about it. Finally, it became routine that, through tears, all Shandy wanted was hot tea and Doctor Nella Merced.

Unlike any other patient Nella had ever had, and very uncharacteristic of her in a professional setting, Nella physically touched Shandy who said it was soothing to hold someone's hand and calming to be near someone. They sat on the couch next to each other drinking tea and sometimes holding hands. Nella let Shandy lay her head on her shoulder or her lap sometimes, stroking her hair lightly or caressing her shoulder. Nella's eyes watered as she sat on the plane thinking about Shandy. She was smart, unique, and full of energy. She laughed but she wasn't happy. She had a big heart with no one to reciprocate the love. She was alone and scared in the world even though she was surrounded by her family. The disease, cancer, like everything else in her life, was her closest ally and greatest enemy.

Nella tried to remember the last time she had seen Shandell. It was an unscheduled meeting. Shandy had come to the office unannounced and without an appointment. She was better she said and was leaving Las Vegas to go to Atlanta. She had finally decided to undergo two of the suggested three rounds of chemotherapy. She said that the tumors were gone, the cancer was gone, and she was 'good to go'. Nella remembered Shandy smiling happily that day, she was talking fast and moving rapidly. Nella herself was getting ready to leave for a conference that she had to attend in Salt Lake City, Utah. She was rushing and Shandy mirrored the haste. Shandy handed Nella a card, gave her a big hug, and thanked her for everything. She said she would never forget Nella and then left.

Nella realized that she had never opened the card. She slipped it into the front pocket of her small carry-on roller bag and hurried to her destination. In the chaos of the weekend conference, she forgot about the card and never thought of it again until this moment. Nella unbuckled her seatbelt and stood up in the aisle. She stretched and then opened the overhead compartment. On her tippy toes, Nella grabbed her bag and pulled it out of the bin, resting it gently on her empty seat. She opened the front pocket and pulled out a large white envelope with a card in it. She zipped the pocket and put the luggage back up into the bin and out of the way. She sat down, refastened her seatbelt, and looked at the envelope. In large cursive letters, Dr. Mercy was scrawled on the front of it. She smiled remembering how Shandy would mimic the Latina accent when she said Merced, sounding very much like mercy. Nella opened the envelope and turned on the light above her head so that she could see more clearly. It read:

> *Thank you so much for your help through this trying time in my life. The doctors think that it was the chemo that made me better, but I know it was the time that I spent with you. Each day in your office drinking hot tea and talking to you gave me just what I needed to overcome this disease. You built me up from the inside out. I know how to love myself now. I know that I don't need to rely on anyone but myself. You Dr. Nella Merced are a saint. An angel. You were God-sent. Thank you so much for the daily doses of love, kindness, and compassion. You saved my life and I am forever grateful to you! You, Dr. Nella will forever be my hot tea and Merced (mercy). Love, Shandy*

In tears, Nella placed the card into her purse which she sat on her lap and hugged to her chest. She tilted her head to the right, leaning it lightly on the headrest of her chair, and fell into a deep slumber, waking only once the lights had come on and the flight attendant on the intercom was asking everyone to fold up their tray tables, bring the backs of their chairs up, and to prepare for landing.

~~~

Eugene's mouth was getting drier by the second. That would have been his primary concern if he could take the attention off the fact that his eyes were blurry and he couldn't see the road he was driving on very well. Up ahead his eyes made out a gas station across the street. He decided that he would make a U-turn at the light and pull into it so that he could buy a bottle of water and sort himself out. As he was approaching the intersection his heart started racing. He began sweating profusely. The light changed from green to yellow, which was perfect timing for the U-turn that he wanted to execute. He lifted the bottom of his shirt up to wipe his forehead and the sweat from his eyes as he rounded the divider.

If he were to have stayed in the lane closest to him, there may not have been a problem. If he had not relied on the power of the red light and looked into his rearview mirror, it may have saved him. However, as Eugene barreled across the two lanes to enter the gas station, he did not notice the eighteen-wheeler that had picked up speed to make it through the yellow light. It was a matter of seconds before the loud sound of metal crashing into and through more metal was heard within a five-block radius. Eugene's body slammed into the driver's side door from the inside of the car, his head smashing through the glass window. He did not feel the airbags deploy, distributing another blow to his face that had swung back inside as his car spun around; he was already dead.

The apologetic truck driver who was caught off-guard by the unexpected car had sustained a few injuries and was taken to the hospital. He was essentially alright and back on the road the following week. With no alcohol in his system and a clean driving record, the truck driver was not arrested for vehicular homicide, though he was ticketed and would have to appear in court at a later date. Video footage from the gas station surveillance cameras would later serve as evidence to prove that he was not at fault for the crash, though the scene of the accident remained forever embedded in his memory, and Eugene's death would haunt him for many years to come.

Eugene was taken directly from the accident to the coroner's office where the cause of death was determined to be blunt trauma to the head as a result of a fatal car accident. If an autopsy would have been performed, the medical examiner would have likely noted that Eugene had suffered a myocardial infarction seconds before his car was struck by the truck. If it was further investigated, the coroner would have found a large amount of ecstasy in his system. Eugene was going to die no matter what, Priscilla had made sure of that. Luckily for him, he died with some dignity in a fatal car crash, rather than as an ecstasy-overdose statistic. Fortunately for Marcella, Eugene's life insurance policy was intact and due to the nature of the accident, wasn't negated by the cause of death.

Marcella did not find out about his death until the following night when one of his family members got in touch with her. She was wrought with sadness and would miss Eugene for the rest of her life, crying for a week straight and anytime she thought about him in the future. Thanks to his life insurance policy, her and the baby would be financially taken care of and though she would never know it, he was better to her dead than alive.

CHAPTER
THIRTY-FIVE

~~~

JOAN RETURNED HOME AFTER her mini-vacation at the hotel. Viraj was furious when she phoned to tell him that she was taking a break and wouldn't be home for the week. He accused her of having an affair with the principal to which she just laughed. She told him he could FaceTime her at any time of the day or night and see that she was by herself but that she needed to be alone for her mental health. She spent the week watching television, taking baths, and getting a massage, manicure, pedicure, and facial. She cried a lot, but that was to be expected. She made new housing arrangements and she called a divorce lawyer. She felt stronger.

Joan stood in front of her closet, eyeing and fingering all of the beautiful clothing that Viraj had bought her. The house was quiet though she was fairly certain that Simone was in the back room. She was unsure where Viraj was at the moment and thought it best not to call him.

Though she had made the definitive decision to leave him, she debated which articles of clothing she should take. She loved all of them but did not feel right or worthy of packing every Armani dress and Jimmy Choo shoe into her Louis Vuitton suitcase set. It was all about perception. She did not want to seem like a gold digger, and she wasn't one. If she only took a few things, she felt, Viraj would know she truly loved him and that his infidelity hurt her to the core. As a materialist, Viraj would feel that Joan actually hated him and was spiting him by leaving all of the expensive gifts he had gotten her.

Joan opened the five-piece Louis set and decided that she would leave whatever could not fit. She filled the largest bag up with her coats, the second largest bag with her shoes, and two of them with her clothes. She reserved the duffle for her photo albums and fragile trinkets that she wanted to take with her. She put some toiletries in a plastic shopping bag and stuffed them in. There was nothing left hanging in her closet, but all of her dresser drawers still had clothes in them. She wasn't too worried about leaving those things behind, tee-shirts, sweatpants, pajamas, underwear. She thought twice about the underwear and tucked them in the sides of each bag along with two pairs of pajamas that would hold her over until she could get to the store. She was pleased with her packing and what she was taking with her. They were hers and she needed them anyway.

Joan rolled each bag to the top of the steps then gave each a slight push with her foot. They slid, tumbled, and cascaded down the flight to the first-floor landing where she then rolled them to the garage to pack her trunk. She was unsure if Simone heard the noise or not, but her sister never came out of the guest room. When Joan had finished loading the car, there was nothing left for her to do but drive off, so that's what she did.

She had planned to leave the garage clicker in the mailbox at the end of the driveway but just as she was reaching to do so, she saw Viraj's car turn the corner. She kept the clicker and maneuvered her car so that they could talk face to face from their driver's side windows. He stopped when he saw her.

"Hey, what's up, where are you going?" He asked, thinking everything was normal.

"I know, Viraj."

"Know what?"

"About you and Simone.

Viraj's face went blank.

"Nothing to say?"

"I don't know what you saw or think you know but I assure you it isn't what you think."

"It is what I think, Viraj."

"Baby, come in the house. Let's talk about it. Is she there? We can clear the air."

"I'm leaving Viraj. I'm leaving this house, this marriage, you. I am leaving and I'm not coming back. You two can have each other. I'm through."

"You're leaving me for your boss?"

"What?"

"Your boss. The principal guy. You're leaving me for him, aren't you?"

"I'm not leaving you because of him. There is no him. I'm leaving you because you are playing me for a fool and sleeping with my sister."

"Please don't go. Please don't go. Just come back to the house and we can talk about it. She can leave. We'll ask her to leave tonight and we can go back to our happy marriage."

"Our marriage isn't happy."

"Please don't leave. You're my wife. I love you."

"I love you too, Viraj. I love you a lot. But I have to love myself. I have to love myself more."

Joan handed him the garage clicker. He attempted to hold her hand but she pulled away. "Goodbye Viraj." She pulled off and left the shocked Viraj sitting in the middle of the cul-de-sac with his mouth open. He couldn't believe what had just happened. He couldn't believe what was happening. His wife just left him, and he had no one to be mad at but himself.

Joan knew where she was headed. She had already reserved a one-month Airbnb stay to give her time to find an apartment that she really liked in a neighborhood she could afford. She called Dr. Nella to make an appointment, but the phone went straight to voicemail. She left a message certain that Dr. Nella would get back to her. There was a calm about Joan. She wasn't angry. She certainly wasn't happy. She was just tired. Not physically tired, but more emotionally drained. She had nothing left to give Viraj and definitely nothing for Simone, not even a goodbye.

CHAPTER THIRTY-SIX

~~~~~

NELLA LANDED AT HARTSFIELD JACKSON at six in the morning, east coast time. It was three a.m. in Las Vegas and she debated calling home. She knew Marcella wouldn't mind the call but didn't want to wake her since she knew how important sleep was to a pregnant woman. Nella's mind ran on Paulo who she had not been able to get in touch with the day before. Surely he was home, but probably asleep. She decided to text them both to say that she had arrived safely in Atlanta and that they could call her when they woke up.

She disembarked the airplane and navigated her way through the large, bright airport that was beginning to bustle with morning activity. She boarded the tram that would take her from where she currently was to where she needed to be, which included baggage claim and ground transportation. With just her purse and her carry-on, she was able to bypass the passengers waiting for their luggage and head directly to the taxi stand after a necessary trip to the ladies' room where she emptied her bladder, brushed her teeth and hair, and applied a fresh, but light coat of lipstick.

It was not hard getting a taxi at that time of the morning on a Sunday. She was third in line and a white and black car pulled up in front of her when it was her turn. The cab driver popped the trunk, but Nella opened the back door and stashed the small carry-on inside, then got in after it. The driver got out of his car, slightly annoyed, to close the trunk and then back to the driver's seat where he looked at Nella through the rearview mirror and asked the inevitable question as he drove off, "Where to, ma'am?"

She read the name of the hotel off of her phone where she had her itinerary email opened. It was a short drive out of the airport and to the hotel. She thanked the driver as she swiped her credit card on the console that sat on the back of the passenger side seat, happy that paying the man was made more convenient by technology. She exited the car, grabbed her suitcase, and pulled the handle up so that she could smoothly roll it alongside her.

Check-in was a breeze. She decided that she would go to her room, shower, dress for the funeral, and then come back downstairs to enjoy the breakfast buffet that the hotel offered. Afterward, she would head to the gravesite to pay her respects to Shandy.

CHAPTER THIRTY-SEVEN

~~~

PRISCILLA HAD DECIDED THAT her daughter was much too
precious to allow her to remain in the streets. Milagro had a chance and
Priscilla did not want her to squander it. Priscilla did a lot of praying
the night that she had poisoned Eugene. Not knowing if her plan had
worked or not, she was terrified that she would be found out and taken
to jail. She knew she had to leave the Merced household. In her mind, it
wouldn't have been long before police officers were swarming the place,
asking questions, searching her room, and interrogating the family. She
didn't sleep all night and at sunrise, she left the house to find the only
person she thought could help her.

Swallowing all her pride, she went back to the area she knew as a
teenager. She asked around for Burger and after a while was directed,
albeit twenty dollars poorer, to the same house she had left nearly twenty
years ago with Milagro in a stroller. She had a small gun in her purse,

which she now transferred to her jacket pocket, another trinket she bought off Fremont Street. She was not planning on using it and didn't even want to possess it but it was part of the arsenal she had acquired for her plan of offing Eugene, and just thought it would come in handy now if Burger wasn't happy to see her. Priscilla knocked on the door. Someone opened it. A woman.

"Can I help you?"

"Hi, I'm here to see Burger."

"Anthony, someone is here to see you."

Priscilla was surprised to hear someone call him Anthony. She had not known Burger's real name until the day Milagro was born and it went onto her birth certificate. She had never called him Anthony and had never heard anyone else ever say his name.

"Who is it?" he said as he approached the door. "Well, I'll be damned."

"Hi."

"Bitch you got me fucked up," was his response.

"I know. I'm sorry. Please hear me out."

"You got thirty seconds."

"Milagro is in trouble. She is wonderful and beautiful and in college but I think she got caught up with some pimp from Fremont and now she is in these streets and you have to get her out. You are the only one who can save our baby girl."

"Oh, she's our baby girl, now?"

"Burger you know I couldn't keep hoeing after she was born. And you know I couldn't stay with you slapping me around."

"What makes you think I won't slap you now?"

"Cause I'll kill you if you do." Priscilla stared at Milagro's father with a seriousness that could not be denied. "I already killed one man who hurt Millie. Now I'm asking you to save her so I don't have to kill another."

With that, Burger opened the door wide so that Priscilla could enter. He wondered what she had been through over the years that had hardened her, his sweetness. He felt a tinge of guilt as his mind ran wild on what he knew awaited so many young girls in the street. He quickly snapped out of it and invited Priscilla to sit at a circular, wooden dining table. Over coffee, she told Burger everything that had happened that summer. As she sat there, Priscilla realized that there was only one woman in the house who had made herself scarce except to fix coffee for the two of them and toast with butter and jelly for Burger. She took her breakfast to the backroom.

"You ain't got no girls?" Priscilla asked matter-of-factly.

"I got a woman. That's all I need."

Priscilla nodded in understanding. "Can you help me find her?"

"Yeah, I can do that."

"I need one more favor."

"Damn you bold."

"We will need to stay here until I can secure some government benefits."

"Real bold."

"It shouldn't take long. If I let them know I'm homeless and have a child, I should be able to get some assistance pretty quickly."

"I have a wife."

"It'll be three weeks, one month tops. I'll go to the benefits office tomorrow. We won't be any trouble."

"Let me talk to her about it. Where is your stuff?"

"I have to go back and get it from the house of the bruja."

"I don't know if you are qualified to call anyone else a witch but, okay. Take my car and do that while I holla at the missus. Take your time coming back, I might need to finesse this situation. As a matter of fact, go grocery shopping for you and Milagro and whatever you think we might need for the house. When you get back, I'll go down to Fremont and see what I can find out."

"Would it be too much to ask for grocery money?"

"Way too much. Take it from the bruja."

"Burger, thank you. But listen, when you go down to Fremont, you know these young guys are different these days. They have guns."

"First of all, you are assuming he's young. Second, I have guns. Third, don't worry, I'll be careful. Now go handle your business so I can handle mine."

Priscilla and Burger got up from the table. He grabbed his keys off the counter and handed them to her. She headed toward the front door then stopped. She turned around to see Burger running his right hand through his hair while the left one propped up his body that was bent over one of the wooden dining chairs. He was older now, still fit but with a little belly that wasn't there before, and still handsome. He was much more mature, which made him all the more attractive.

"Thank you, Burger."

"You're welcome. And call me Anthony, I don't go by Burger anymore."

Priscilla smiled and turned to leave the house. When she got outside, she took a deep breath and for the first time in weeks felt like things would be alright. With a few clicks of the panic button, she found Anthony's car and was surprised to see that he was driving a Hyundai Genesis. It was sleek and very sexy. She smiled again at how much Burger had grown over the years. She wondered where that guy was when she met him. And married. She was proud of him and happy for him. She knew that he didn't have to do anything that she was asking of him. He was doing it because he loved her, and he loved Milagro. She genuinely appreciated him and knew that she owed him for this, so in return, she would do exactly as she told him she would, get herself together and get out of there as soon as she could.

CHAPTER THIRTY-EIGHT

≋

PRISCILLA PULLED UP TO the Merced residence. It was late afternoon and still warm outside. She went directly to her room to pack her belongings. It was quiet. After filling the two suitcases that she arrived with, she still had a few things hanging in the closet, two pairs of shoes, and a draw of pajamas. She was surprised at how much extra clothing she had acquired since being there, although some of it may have been left behind by her daughter. Not wanting to waste any more time, Priscilla went to the kitchen to retrieve a large garbage bag. She threw the rest of her stuff in it and took everything out to the car. After she placed the bags in the trunk, she went back into the house to raid the pantry and refrigerator for food.

Standing in front of the cupboards, Priscilla felt like Old Mother Hubbard. She realized it was Sunday, the day Paulo usually went grocery shopping, but he hadn't gone yet. His car was in the driveway so Priscilla knew he was home. She would have to ask him for some money, something that would not be hard to get out of him if she had a good excuse. She thought about what she would say the money was for as she walked down the hallway to his bedroom. As she approached, she could hear the television on cartoons. That meant one of two things, Paulo was either in the shower or taking a nap and the T.V. was babysitting Angel.

Priscilla scurried back to the kitchen to retrieve three cookies for Angel, which she placed on a paper towel in front of him as he sat on the bed watching television. It was just her luck that Paulo was asleep. His wallet was on the dresser, so she quietly took the two one-hundred-dollar bills that were nestled inside. She then stealthily opened the top drawer of Nella's armoire just slightly and squiggled her hand around underneath the panties until she found the wad of cash she knew her patrona kept there. Without stopping to count it, she made her way down the hallway as if she was floating on air. She looked around her bedroom and thought about anything else she may have been forgetting. There was nothing. She placed the house keys on top of her dresser, closed the bedroom door, and headed out of the house.

As she went to put the key in the ignition, she realized that her hands were shaking. She was hot and sweaty, and her mouth was dry. She pulled off and only decided to count the money she retrieved from Nella's drawer once she pulled into a parking spot at the grocery store. Nella would certainly miss the fifteen-hundred dollars that Priscilla came upon. She allocated three hundred dollars for groceries including paper towels, toilet paper, and anything else she could think of that would make their stay more comfortable at Burger's. She just hoped his wife would be okay with them being there. Then she hoped Burger would be able to find Milagro and bring her home. Before Priscilla got out of the car, she pulled out her cell phone to make a call. There was one final thing she had to do to cut ties with the Mercedes.

CHAPTER
THIRTY-NINE

The Funeral

THE SERVICE WAS LIGHTLY attended, but beautiful, nonetheless. A large picture of Shandell stood on an easel next to the already dug grave and her casket sat atop a machine that would lower it into the ground once everything was over. Nella had never been to a graveside funeral but figured this was how they did things in the south. The minister asked if anyone wanted to speak and Shandell's son surprisingly approached the microphone.

"My name is Raphael, Jr. and I am Shandell's first son. No one but a select few people knew that she was my biological mother because she gave me up for adoption when I was just two weeks old. I didn't even know this until a few years ago, when my mother, her aunt, was sick on her deathbed and told me. People cannot just have children because they think it will be cute. Babies are not toys or playthings. Babies are real. They are people and they grow up to become adults. When children are mistreated, misguided, misunderstood, they become misfits. I was a misfit. I am a misfit. Perhaps my mother, Shandell, was too. Parents, you have to do better at loving your children. And not just with a roof over their heads, food on the table, and clothes on their backs. They have to be acknowledged, paid attention to, hugged, and loved. Loved in a way that we know we are loved and there is no doubt in our minds. Children have to be wanted. We must be a forethought, not an afterthought. Children are not accidents."

As Raphael, Jr. continued his soliloquy about children and parenthood, Nella's phone rang. She hurriedly fished it out of her purse to silence it and realized it was Priscilla calling. Not wanting to be rude but concerned it might be something with Angel, Nella picked up the call and stepped away from the small crowd that was gathered by the graveside.

"Hello, Pri. Is everything okay?"

"Hola Nella. Yes, everything is okay. Angel is watching cartoons while Paulo sleeps."

"And Marcella?"

"I don't know where she is. I am calling about something else," Priscilla's voice began to shake.

"Can it wait? I am at the funeral."

"It will only take a second." Priscilla did not want to prolong this uncomfortable conversation. She did not know what to say or how to say it. She closed her eyes and thought about Milagro leaving in the middle of the night. She thought about Nella's coldness, her strict rules, and her cruel words.

"Okay, go ahead, I'm listening," Nella's voice jolted Priscilla out of her thoughts.

"I quit."

The phone went silent before Nella could respond. A little stunned by this revelation, Nella began to feel hot and weak. She decided to get through the rest of the funeral before she called Paulo. She would return home that evening and sort things out once she got there.

"Thank you, brother Raphael. Who else would like to speak?" the minister asked as Nella reapproached the group. "Very good there, young lady, come on up."

Nella realized he was speaking to her, and everyone was looking. She was not prepared for this. She gestured with her hand to indicate that she was not interested in approaching the microphone, but the minister was insistent. A few others in the crowd encouraged her and gestured with their hands for her to go forward. She acquiesced and with wobbly legs, approached the mic.

Nella began, "I am doctor Marianella Merced. I am a psychiatrist and Shandell was a client of mine. She began coming to see me when she was sick with cancer, just to talk. She was a special woman. She had her struggles but was kind and caring. She loved all of her children and deeply regretted being forced to give up her son. I remember when she told me that. She wanted to keep the baby, but her parents made her give him to her barren aunt so that she could finish high school. I am not sure if she ever did finish. She sunk into a depression that never left her. She found comfort in food which then became her biggest enemy over the years. Shandell herself was misguided, misunderstood, felt mistreated, and indeed became a misfit in her mind.

"Shandy wanted to love life but did not know how. In the days that she came to see me, we would drink tea and talk about life and love, peace and happiness, poverty and sadness. We would talk about aliens and sea creatures. Sometimes we would talk about ghosts and demons. Shandy was very intelligent and beautiful. We would hold hands," Nella's eyes began to tear up and her voice wavered. "Sometimes we just sat in silence. She called me Dr. Mercy. We would sit, talk, sip tea, and heal together. I remember one day she came in very upset and asked me to make a pot of tea, not just a cup, a whole pot. She asked me to sit next to her and she moved close enough to me so that our feet touched, side by side. She sat back and drank tea with her eyes closed. Three cups. She never said anything and then the session was over. She said thank you and hugged me. As she was leaving, I told her the point of coming to therapy was to talk and she said, 'No Dr. Mercy, I don't come here just to talk. I come here for hot tea and you. You are my mercy.' Then she left. May she rest in peace and be filled with hot tea and mercy wherever she is."

Everyone was crying. There wasn't a dry eye at the graveside. "Thank you, sister Mercy. Would anyone else like to come up and say a few words about sister Shandell Wright O'Brien?" The minister had taken his place back at the microphone and was once again calling up family and friends.

Nella decided it was a good time to make her departure. The service was practically over, and she did not feel like talking to a bunch of strangers who were sure to come up and speak to her afterward now that they knew who she was. She walked to the hired car and changed her flight as she made her way to the hotel to retrieve her bag and then on to the airport to wait. She would be early, which would give her time to settle her nerves and call Paulo to find out what happened. As she rode through the almost empty streets of Atlanta that Sunday afternoon, she began to cry. By the time she reached the airport, she was sobbing uncontrollably. Nella cried for Shandell, she cried for her son, Angel, she cried for Priscilla, and she cried for herself.

~~~~

"Take me to the airport, I want to go home now," Mrs. Wright was furious.

"Grandma, your flight isn't even until Thursday," Kayla said as she held her smallest child in one arm while scrambling eggs with the other.

The rest of the previous evening went by in a blur, shaking hands, hugging, thanking people for coming to the funeral, and accepting their condolences. By the time the last guest left the repast and all of the leftover food was put away, everyone was exhausted and all anyone could do was change into their pajamas, climb into bed, and fall into a deep sleep. The next morning, however, Mrs. Wright sat at the kitchen table complaining about Nella's speech and the embarrassment it caused her and the family.

"Can you believe that hussy? Telling all of our business. Like she even knew Shandell that well. She doesn't even know what she is talking about. She lied. Got up there and just lied and lied and lied. I want to go home."

"Grandma, I don't think that lady lied. I think she shared with us what my mom told her in privacy. I don't think it was right for her to tell all her business like that, but it was good for us to hear the truth. To know the truth that we may have never known."

"The truth? The truth? If you are saying that lady told the truth, then you are calling me a liar."

"You are a liar, grandma," Raphael, Jr. entered the kitchen fresh out of the shower. "That smells good."

"How dare you?"

"How dare you? I hated my mother until the day she died because of your lies and my other mother's lies. Now I'll never be able to fix it. My mother died thinking I hated her when all these years, all these years," Raphael, Jr. could not bring himself to say it. He was mad at his grandmother, but he did not want to crush her.

"Shut your mouth," Mrs. Wright snapped.

Kayla put toast and eggs on a plate and held it out to her brother.

"Grandma, you stole me from my mother. Don't ever tell me to shut my mouth again. Thank you," he took the plate from Kayla and left the kitchen to eat his food while he watched television in the living room.

Kayla sat a plate on the table in front of her grandmother. "I'm not hungry, I want to go home."

"Change your ticket," Raphael, Jr. yelled from the living room. "I'll take you to the airport."

With that, Mrs. Wright went to pack her bags and call the airlines to change her ticket for the first flight she could get out of Atlanta and back to Las Vegas. Kayla put the sleeping baby in his crib and sat down at the table to eat her breakfast but all she ended up doing was cry. Having completely spaced out, it was about an hour later when she heard movement. Her grandmother was bringing her suitcase out of the room, the baby was crying, and Raphael was hugging Kayla goodbye.

She said goodbye to her grandmother, picked up the baby, and sat down on her bed. It was quiet for the first time in a long time. It was too quiet. The thoughts in her head became loud. Her anger was audible. Her sadness was deafening. Kayla was in the perfect storm and she could feel the depression coming on. She put the baby next to her on the bed and called Bobby so that he could pick the other boys up from school. She wouldn't be getting out of bed for the rest of the day.

CHAPTER FORTY

Sister-Sister

〜〜〜

"HEY, PRINCESS SIMONE, do you think you can make yourself useful around here today, maybe fold the towels that are in the dryer or wash the dishes," Viraj was visibly annoyed as he stood in the doorway to her bedroom.

"I don't do dishes," Simone retorted as she sat on her bed eating potato chips.

"You don't do dishes? Well, what do you do besides smoke up my weed, sleep, watch t.v., and eat?"

She muted the television with the remote. "Oh please, I do plenty."

"Please tell me. Tell me what you do."

"I make my bed, I keep my bathroom clean, I fluff the pillows on the couch."

"Are you serious, right now? There's a garbage bin full of your takeout boxes that needs to be taken."

"I don't take out the trash."

Viraj's voice went low, "You don't take the trash, huh? You don't take the trash?" In an instant of fury, Viraj turned and punched the wall leaving a hole the size of his fist in it. Simone jumped. "You got it twisted if you think you can just sit around here and mooch off me. Your sister left me and I'll be damned if I'm going to take care of you. I'm going to the strip club for a few hours, be gone by the time I get back."

"Gone? Where am I supposed to go?"

"I don't know, but you got to get the hell outta here."

Viraj left Simone's room without another word and in seconds she could hear his car peeling down the driveway.

"Damn," she said to herself. "What am I supposed to do now?"

Simone didn't even know that Joan had left Viraj. She knew it was quieter than usual, but she was just keeping to herself in the backroom and thought Joan was either at work or asleep when she did come out. She decided to call her. The phone rang once, twice, then was sent to voicemail. A knot formed in the pit of Simone's stomach. Did Joan know? Did Viraj tell her? Was Joan not speaking to her?

Simone realized the severity of the situation and began to cry. Slowly, she crawled out of bed and began to pack her things. Maybe she would take a Lyft to the airport and spend the night there until she figured out where she was going and booked a flight. She hated to think about it, but if she didn't have a place to go by morning, she would have to call Lou and tell him she was coming home. She reconsidered the airport and decided to have the Lyft take her to the bus station.

Joan was grading papers when her phone rang. She looked at the screen and saw it was her sister, Simone calling. Decline. Joan shook her head in disbelief that her sister would call her and for the fact that it took her this long to call in the first place. No message, no text. Was she even calling to apologize? Did she even know Joan was gone? Joan tried to keep her mind calm so that she could finish grading.

Work was going well and she secured an apartment that she would move into at the beginning of the following month. Life was good even though she missed Viraj quite a bit. She missed having someone to sleep next to and she missed cooking for him. In time she knew the longing to talk to him and be in his arms would subside. She cried sometimes and prayed often. She immersed herself in her work and she scheduled regular sessions to speak with Dr. Nella. She remedied those unbearable nights when loneliness crept in and she felt the pressure of lost love building up, with a vibrator.

CHAPTER FORTY-ONE

~~~

NELLA RETURNED HOME TO FIND Marcella holding Angel in her lap, squeezing him tightly, rocking back and forth, sobbing.

"Hermana, ¿que paso? What happened? Is everything okay?" Nella dropped her bags and quickly approached her sister, taking Angel out of her arms and examining him thoroughly.

"He's dead."

"Who's dead?" Nella began to panic, "Marcella tell me, who is dead?"

"Eugene. He died in a car accident."

"¿Un accidente?"

"Si, hermana. Un accidente. Ahora, esta muerto."

"Dead?" Nella stood frozen. Her feet were stuck to the floor and she couldn't move. She was stunned at this news. She had so many questions: When? How? Where? She had just seen him. She had just kissed him. She couldn't believe he was gone. Immediately she felt guilty. She felt that

God took Eugene's life because of the other night at the airport. She felt sick to her stomach. If God had punished Eugene, she would surely be next. "I will make some tea for us. Let me put Angel to bed."

Nella hugged Angel for a long time and then laid him in his bed. She kissed him good night and turned the television to the cartoon network for his comfort. She dragged her bags to her room and then went to the kitchen to make peppermint tea. She stood over the sink listening to the water boil. She thought of Eugene. His hands, his mouth, his smell. She leaned her head back to prevent the tears from forming. It was to no avail as they began to roll down her cheeks. The kettle whistled.

"¿Donde esta Paulo?" Nella asked her sister as she entered the room with two mugs of tea.

"I'm not sure where Paulo is. He went grocery shopping hours ago."

"Let me call him," Nella put her mug down and went to fetch her phone from the purse in her room. She dialed his number.

"Hello Nella, are you back?"

"Yes, I'm home. Where are you?"

"I'm headed home from the grocery store."

"So late?"

"I'm just around the corner. I came earlier but there was a mix up. Once everything was rung up there was no cash in my wallet, even though I know I had two-hundred dollars in there. Anyway, I'll be home shortly."

"What happened to the money that was in your wallet?"

"I don't know. And I don't know where Priscilla has been all day."

"Oh yeah, she quit."

"Quit, Dios Mio. I'll be home shortly."

"Okay, bye." Nella slowly made her way back to Marcella's room thinking what a mess everything was. Then, a thought came to her. Priscilla may have stolen Paulo's money before she left. Nella spun on her heels back to her room and opened the top drawer of her armoire. She rifled through it, finally pulling everything out and realizing that her money was gone, all fifteen hundred of it. Maybe she put it in another drawer. She began searching through all of her drawers, then Paulo's. She found nothing. She looked through the nightstand on her side of the bed, then rolled across to the other side and went through Paulo's stand.

As she rummaged through his drawer, she realized she had never opened it before. Tylenol, sleeping pills, receipts, a mini flashlight. "Such a nerd," she giggled to herself.

Paulo began bringing groceries into the house and called out for some help. Nella was about to close the drawer when a plain, manilla folder caught her eye. She picked it up and opened it. She pulled out the contents of freshly printed papers which sported a Med Care logo. She looked at the recent date and scanned down the columns. There were letters and numbers and ranges and HIV, positive. Nella dropped the papers and fainted.

~~~~~~

"Is anyone going to help me with these groceries?" Paulo asked as he came down the hallway, peering into Marcella's room first and then his own. "Nella, Nella are you, okay?" He rushed to the bed and kicked the papers on the floor. "Oh no. Oh no. Nella, Nella, NELLA."

Nella stirred. "Paulo, are you sick?"

"That's what the paper says."

"I have to get tested."

"We don't even have sex, Nella."

"But we did. We did Paulo, and now I could be sick."

"I'm sorry."

"It's God's punishment. Dios Mio, I'm sorry," Nella began to cry.

"I'm going to put the groceries away."

"I have to get Angel tested."

"That's ridiculous, he couldn't have it."

"Not for that, for autism."

Paulo paused. "The groceries," he muttered and left the room.

Nella got down on her knees to pray. She prayed for Eugene's soul. She prayed for Marcella and the unborn baby. She prayed for Paulo, Angel, and herself. She prayed for Joan. She prayed for Shandy's family. She prayed for all of her clients. After she said amen and got up, she realized she forgot someone. She picked up her phone and scrolled through her contacts. She called her good friend Antonio, Marcella's ex-boyfriend. Since it went to voicemail, she decided to leave a message.

"Hola amigo. I just found out some crazy news. Schedule to get an HIV test as soon as you can. I'm sorry. We'll talk manana. I'm sorry. Good night."

CHAPTER
FORTY-TWO

～～～

IT WAS ALL SAINTS DAY and people from all over Las Vegas were filing into the Sunrise International Spiritual Center. It was a large, cathedral-like building that hosted pictures of Jesus, Muhammad, Gandhi, Mother Theresa, and the Dalai Lama on the walls. People of all faiths worshiped there regularly under the non-denominational reverend, whose main message was one of love, peace, and unity.

Priscilla took a seat close to the wall in a row that was semi-empty, though she knew it would fill up sooner than not. Though she was not a devout Catholic, like many Latinas, she grew up in the Catholic church and never missed the events surrounding the Saints. She wore her Rosary and was lost in thoughtful prayer as the church filled up. The seat next to her remained empty since her bible currently occupied it and she didn't hear when three different people asked her if the seat was taken.

Although Milagro still wasn't home, Priscilla was grateful that she was able to find a cheap two-bedroom apartment on the Northeast side of Vegas. It wasn't in the best neighborhood, but she wasn't worried about that. With the money she nabbed from Nella's drawer, she was able to pay the first month's rent and security. She was sure she would find a job before the next rent payment was due. She would be alright as long as Milagro came home. She needed her daughter back.

Burger drove around the surrounding streets of Fremont looking for his daughter. He had gone out almost every day for a month at different times but hadn't found her. He did recently get the name Rollo. On one of those days in the earlier weeks, he pulled over and began to laugh realizing that he didn't even know what Milagro looked like. His laughter turned into tears thinking about all of the women he had put on the stroll. He had already come to terms with his past but the fact that it came back to haunt him was distressing. He had hoped he would be able to find her without having to do too much prying in the streets but on this brisk Sunday morning, he decided to enter a diner that was known for lascivious activity. He figured he would at least be able to find out if his daughter was a junkie, whore, or both if he showed the picture he obtained from Priscilla to the waitstaff.

Mrs. Wright and Kayla were ushered down the aisle to a row with enough seats for them and Kayla's children. With too much on her mind in Atlanta, she decided to put in a temporary leave of absence with her job and visit her grandmother in Las Vegas to get away for a while. Her grandmother told her that she was welcome to stay for as long as she wanted and that there was plenty of room for them if they wanted to move altogether. Kayla was toying with the idea but had not made any definitive decisions yet.

Joan was invited to attend the All Saints service by her boss. She had declined at first but he convinced her that it would do her some good to hear the word of God. Joan protested that she wasn't even Christian but he assured her that the place of worship was all-inclusive and the love of God was non-denominational. With a lawyer drawing up the no-contest divorce papers, and still no word to or from her sister, she agreed to have a little of God's love showered on her, even if she didn't believe in Christ or the Saints.

Burger walked into the diner and to his surprise saw the same cook in the kitchen all these years later. "Big Mac, is that you?"

"Who dat is?"

"Burger."

"Big Burger, well I'll be damned. Look at you all growed up."

"Man, it's great to see you."

"Likewise. You still in the game?"

"Aw nah man. Been got out. Settled down, got me an ole lady at home."

"That's good, Burger, that's real good. I'll have Sue come take your order."

"Actually, I'm here on some business."

"What kind of business."

"I'm looking for a girl. My daughter actually. She got hooked up with some guy down here a few weeks back and got her mother goin' crazy. I'm here to find her, make sure she alright. You know a guy named Rollo?"

Mac didn't say anything but just gestured to a man sitting at a corner table by the window. There were three women in the booth with him, two with their backs to Burger. Burger placed a twenty-dollar bill on the counter and slowly got off the barstool he sat on.

"It was great seeing you man."

"Drop in anytime."

Burger slowly made his way to Rollo's table. Though he had a gun in his pocket he attempted to look and sound as non-threatening as possible.

"Hey brother, I hear you're Rollo and I've been looking for you to have a word." As Burger approached the table, the faces of the other two women became visible. One he recognized. "Millie."

She looked up at the unfamiliar face. "Do I know you?"

"I'm your father."

Nella, Paulo, Angel, and Marcella took seats on the upstairs balcony. Tension among them had subsided over the week and things were mostly back to normal in their household. Although she hadn't heard from Antonio since she left the message, Nella was relieved that her test came back negative. She silently thanked God as she remembered her promise to Him in a fervent prayer the morning she went to take her HIV test. She would have to sign up for alcoholics anonymous and quit drinking to hold up her end of the bargain since God certainly held up His.

There would be some major changes in the Merced household. Besides the upcoming arrival of Marcella's baby girl, Paulo had asked Nella for a referral to see a psychiatrist of his own. He thought it would be a good idea to seek professional help to work through some of his past trauma and current problems, including his recent diagnosis. Nella agreed and gave him a list of a few doctors who she did not know personally. She also searched for some reputable marriage counselors that they could start seeing after they got Angel on track. Nella and Paulo were still coming to terms with Angel's autism diagnosis. Angel would be seeing a specialist in the upcoming weeks to design a program for his development, and Paulo and Nella had already joined a support group for parents of children with autism. They would get through it together and be stronger for it.

As a final good-faith gesture, Nella drafted a letter to the American Psychiatric Association to formally surrender her license for three years while she addressed personal issues and completed a course for teaching ethics at the local community college. Even if she never became a professor, at least she would again be competent in the code of ethics and regulations that she was sworn to.

The reverend came on stage, approached the podium, and began speaking into the microphone:

Ladies and gentlemen if you would please take your seats. I thank you so much for being here today. The Universe thanks you. Cosmic forces

thank you. The Most High thanks you. And you should thank your-
selves and your neighbor for being here in the right place at the right
time on this day. This is a day that celebrates love. A love so great that
God created not one but many who watch over us, have our backs, set
an example for us to follow, protect us and our children, and answer
our prayers. The Saints. Think about that for a moment, congregation.
Who in your life right now would be willing to give up everything for
you? Who in this world would you be willing to give up everything you
have for? Your house, your car, your clothes, your job? Is there anyone
you would do that for? That isn't an easy question if you're honest with
yourself, yet the Christ in his superior consciousness died for your sins
so that you may be saved and have life through him. And the Saints
follow his example. We are all sinners, and we were all saved. No man
or woman is better than the next one regardless of shape, color, height,
race, bank account, ethnicity, language, occupation, marital status, or
anything. We are equal in God's eyes and cannot judge one another. Let
he that hath not sinned be the first to cast stones - Amen. Let he that
hath done no wrong in God's eyes point out the wrongs of his brother.
Can you pull that camel through the eye of a needle? I ask you again,
congregation, who here can pull...

Priscilla's phone vibrated in the purse on her lap. She fished it out and saw
a text from Burger telling her to come outside. Annoyed by the interrup-
tion at church, she debated making him wait since the reverend was right
in the middle of his sermon and she didn't want to walk past the whole
row of people to make her way to the aisle. Her phone began to vibrate
uncontrollably with Burger now calling her.

She answered and whispered into the phone, "I'll be right there."
She regretted having texted him the night before to ask if he and his wife
wanted to attend with her. Even though they all had lived harmoniously
together for the few weeks that she lived with them, they weren't exactly
friends. Burger declined the invitation in a text message, not because they
didn't like Priscilla, but it was more that they didn't like church.

Priscilla made her way out of the main hall into the lobby of the church and fell to her knees in tears when she saw her daughter standing there. Millie walked over to her mother and helped her off the floor. They hugged.

"Where's your dad?"

"He left. I am coming home with you tonight."

"To stay?"

"I think so."

"I'm glad. Milagro, I love you, mija. You are my everything and I'm sorry, so sorry."

"It's okay ma, I love you too."

"I left Nella's. I don't work there anymore. And don't worry about Eugene. He will never hurt you again. I'm sorry, mija. Please forgive me."

"Of course, I forgive you ma. Wipe your face. Let's go inside."

The two went back into the main hall. Priscilla took her seat and Millie moved the bible and sat next to her mother. They held hands for the rest of the sermon, Priscilla lost in the words and Milagro lost in her thoughts.

Joan's boss took her to a lovely lunch after the church service. They had a nice time and talked about things outside of the school building, which was a welcomed change. He expressed interest in her, off the record, to which she admitted she was flattered but could not accept his advances so fresh out of a relationship. She was indeed still married and needed time to divorce, heal, and be by herself for a while. He said that he understood and wanted her to know that he respected her and considered her a friend. He made it clear that the invitation was always open and until then she could consider him a willing ear or shoulder anytime she needed one. Joan was truly grateful and verbally expressed her appreciation.

She had received a text message from Simone while she was out. Although she noticed it, she had not bothered to open or think about it until she had gotten home, changed her clothes, and poured herself a glass of red wine. She had neither heard from nor reached out to Simone since the last time she ignored Simone's call. She didn't know where she was or what was going on with her. She thought about her sister often and their dismal relationship bothered her. She opened the text message and it simply said *I'm sorry*. Joan without even having to think about it simply replied, *I forgive you*. At the same time, each sister sent and received a text that stated *I love you*.

After church, each family went to their respective homes to enjoy supper together. Perhaps it was the reverend's sermon about the sacrifice that Jesus and the Saints made or the idea that God loved the world so much that he gave his only begotten son. Or maybe everyone was exhausted over all of the chaos of the year, the pain, the loss, the betrayal, the hurt, as well as the healing, the love, and the inner calm that the weathered storms had brought about. Whatever the reason, there were no arguments that evening. There were no grudges, no mean words, no evil eyes. It was just food, fun, and faith. Things weren't perfect and never would be, but they would always be family, always.

RAE LASHEA is a Brooklyn-born author who travels extensively to experience the world through the eyes of those who are often invisible. She has immersed herself in the international culture, customs, and cuisine of 30+ countries, including Kenya where she lived among the Masai. Her current publications include *Black Geisha*, *You Are a Star*, and *52 Weeks of MIRACLES*, as well as the short film *Filly*. As a social anthropologist and former special education teacher, Rae believes in the power of being a life-long learner and doing your own research. She currently resides in the United States.

lessproblemsmoremiracles.com
instagram.com/raelashea

Forget Her
by Holly Riordan

The Poet's Girl,
A Novel of Emily Hale & T.S. Eliot
by Sara Fitzgerald

When You're Ready, This Is How You Heal
by Brianna Wiest

From Excuses to Excursions:
How I Started Traveling the World
by Gloria Atanmo

What I Wish I Knew About Love
by Kirstie Taylor

**THOUGHT
CATALOG**
Books

THOUGHTCATALOG.COM